I0623271

# GRIMWEAVE

## TIM CURRAN

SEVERED PRESS
HOBART TASMANIA

GRIMWEAVE

**WWW.SEVEREDPRESS.COM**

**ISBN: 978-1-925342-12-3**

1

The bodies were scattered over the ground in jackstraw heaps. They were all dressed identically in black pajamas, Ho Chi Minh sandals, and boonie hats. Their limbs were sprawled in crazy, unnatural positions. The sort of positions only death could inspire. Most had their faces blown off; a few were missing the tops of their heads. A couple others took it in the back where the hollow-tip slugs had shattered their spines into shrapnel. Those were pretty shots when you could get them.

"Nothing much here, Gunny," Spiers said, checking over the bodies for maps, weapons, and personal effects.

Carmody stood there, still as stone, rivulets of perspiration running down his green-streaked face. He spat on one of the bodies. "I want that officer," he said. He'd been saying it over and over again since they'd drilled the others and the officer had slipped away like an eel on glass. It was his mantra: "I want that fucking officer."

"He won't get far, gut-shot like that. He's probably tripping over his intestines as we speak. Sure as shit."

"You don't know that."

"I saw it through the scope."

"You didn't see shit."

"I did."

Carmody pushed his peaked camo cap from his sweat-beaded brow. He licked his dirty lips. They tasted like salt and loam and cordite. "You saw it through the scope, Cherry? Is that what you're telling me? Is that the flavor of the fucking day?"

Spiers shook his head, leafing through wrinkled, stained photographs he'd taken off the dead Cong. They were pictures of girlfriends. They looked like hookers and bar girls from Saigon. For some reason, he always thought they'd look different. He stuffed them in his rucksack.

"C'mon, Gunny," he said. "I been in-country eight months, I ain't no cherry."

Carmody laughed. "Eight months? *Eight fucking months?* You're a cherry with a tiny tee-tee pecker, son. You ain't never sunk your meat into the serious shit. You barely even popped your bone yet. This is my third tour. You do three tours, shitbug, you know what real fucking's all about. Takes three tours to get your balls hard. After three goddamn ass-busting tours you know what it's like to get fucked by the system good and proper."

Spiers sighed, lit a cigarette. "Yeah, okay, here we go. Thirty years in the Corps. Bougainville. Okinawa. Frozen Chosin. Hue. Khe Sanh. I've heard it all before, Gunny. Shit, you're the man. You're all John Wayne."

*"John Wayne?* Now don't insult me by comparing me with some Hollywood faggot that never even served. John Wayne wouldn't know one end of an assault rifle from the other, goddammit. He squats to piss."

"I was just kidding you, Gunny."

"Try and make it funny next time so we can all have a laugh."

"Roger that."

Carmody laughed again. "That's what I like about you, Cherry. You ain't got no respect for no one. Hell kind of Marine are you anyway? I get the feeling that there's a hippy inside you trying to get out. That you'd wipe your ass with the flag and burn your bra if I let you."

"Well, my tits do get kind of sweaty in this heat, Gunny."

Carmody scowled at him.

Spiers smiled thinly, knowing that few dared. Carmody was boocoo insane. He liked hurting people; it was what he was good at. Once you got to know him, Spiers figured, he wasn't so bad. You just had to overlook the body count he left lying around. Like a pet snake, you just had to be aware of his bite.

Spiers sighed. "These slopes ain't got nothing worth a shit, Gunny." He kicked the pile of AK-47s he'd gathered from the corpses. "Not even an SKS in the lot. I'd give my right testicle for an SKS. Every time we go out hunting, I think, yeah, today's the day I'm going to get me an SKS, but I never get one."

The SKS was a Soviet semi-auto rifle that Spiers had been salivating over for months. He wasn't sure why he had to have one, other than the fact that he couldn't seem to get one.

2

Carmody turned his gaze from the treeline. "Yeah, yeah, you and your goddamn SKS. And who told you the smoking lamp was lit? Put that sumbitch out. Slopes can smell American tobacco for miles."

"I was done anyway." Spiers butted it on the damp sole of his jungle boot. He buried it in the soft earth so no one would find an American cigarette butt lying around.

Carmody slipped his cap off and swatted flies with it, scratching his bristly gray scalp with his other hand. Using the spotting scope, he scanned the jungle in all directions. He frowned, cussed, shook his head. "If that gook officer was gut-shot, he sure made a good run of it."

"He's dying. Gotta be. He probably dropped dead out there somewhere. We'll never find him. You know how they go to ground."

"Less talking, Suzie Q. Fix those weapons."

Spiers went about sabotaging the AKs. It was SOP. If you couldn't take it with you, you denied the enemy the use of it. In the case of rifles, you rigged them so they'd explode next time they were fired. Denying the enemy got carried to great extremes like everything in that war. The infantry would generally destroy anything it couldn't carry off—burn hootches, blow ammo dumps, booby trap enemy dead, shoot pigs and chickens and dogs, torch crops. There was an art form to total destruction and there was no more dangerous, brutal animal in the world than a nineteen-year-old American boy. Spiers had heard that some of the soldier of fortune snake-eaters—SEALs and LRRPs and Berets—would actually drop poison vials into wells and inject livestock with infectious diseases. Maybe it was just bullshit, but maybe not. The stories made the rounds and you tried not to think too much about them.

Spiers and Carmody were a sniper team, spotter and shooter, though they both did their fair share of both. There wasn't much they could do to deny the enemy besides putting bullets in their skulls. Today had been a good kill: six Viet Cong sappers. Easy as pie. They caught them in a dry wash and picked them off one by one. They both did the hunting. They set up in a high bamboo thicket and started popping rounds before the VC knew what was what. It had almost been too easy: nice clean headshots for the most part.

It got to Spiers every time.

The way the body flopped around, the brain going haywire and shooting electricity down every neural pathway, energizing every single nerve ending. It was obscene for a man to die like that, flipping and jumping and writhing...yet, *intriguing*. Like a sideshow attraction that disgusted you, but made you look. No dignity in a death like that.

Carmody had taken out two of them in that manner.

The gooks had been asking for it, really, getting themselves tangled up in a clusterfuck like that. Out in the open, sitting around sucking up their fish sauce and rice. Uncle Ho should've thanked Carmody and Spiers for greasing the bastards. After the shooting was over, Carmody lobbed a grenade into the wash to finish the job. It hadn't been necessary, but Carmody was nothing if not thorough.

But somehow, some way, that officer had slipped away. Go figure. Those Viets could be god-awful tenacious when the mood struck them.

Spiers could see him now—the canvas belt he wore, the red star emblazoned on the square aluminum belt buckle. An officer, all right. He'd seen him go down, seen that round—one of Carmody's—clip him in the belly.

Yet, he'd made a run of it.

Amazing.

Not for the first time, Spiers was absolutely in awe of the human will to survive.

"We better E and E our asses out of here, Gunny," he said, feeling uneasy for some reason. The sun. The heat. The dank, rotting undergrowth...he wasn't sure what. "Let's escape and evade and find that LZ before dark. We don't wanna be left out here."

Carmody got that look on his face. "I think we're gonna track that gook officer, Cherry."

*Shit,* Spiers thought, *there goes my drunk. Carmody...fucking boonie-rat Jungle Jim manhunter.*

He licked salt off his lips. "Maybe we shouldn't, Gunny. That dink probably made for a base camp. We ain't up to tangling with a VC/NVA company tonight."

"Don't be such a pussy, Cherry. There's no camp out there. Ain't no nothing out there. No Charlies. Not even Tarzan. Just one belly-shot slope that I plan to finish off. Fucker'll probably be dead by the time we find him."

But Spiers just shook his head. "He went east for chrissake. Probably making for the Cambode border to meet his buddies. And, shit, we can't be far from there now. You know we can't go over the fence. You know that well as I do."

"Says who?"

"Regulations. Rules of engagement—"

"Fuck regulations, Cherry," Carmody spat. "I want that little zipperhead. I plan to mount his sorry head on my wall. Besides, we're an easy twelve klicks from the border. We'll tag that bitch in two. Probably fell into the bush and died."

Spiers said, "We ain't no twelve klicks, Gunny. We're way the hell out here. I never been out this far before. Border is probably just over that rise. We get caught there—"

"Be better if we were caught here?"

Spiers just shook his head. "The chopper…"

"Don't sweat that, Cherry. They know how I work. Nobody pops smoke, they won't even come in. They'll come back in the morning and we'll be waiting for 'em."

"Ah, Gunny, c'mon…I need a cold beer."

"Fuck you and your cold beer, sweet Mary Jane."

Spiers rubbed his eyes. He needed this like tits and a wiggle. It had WIA or KIA written all over it. And, maybe worse, *POW.* He knew it would happen, though. Carmody was one crazy gung ho grunt. A diddy-bopping bloodhound. Usually, they went out as a five-man Killer Team—Carmody, Spiers, two grunts, a radioman. But when it was just the two of them like this, Carmody acted like they were out on a father and son camping trip. Fucking boy scouts hiking out to Camp Pokatwatta.

But it was pointless to argue; Carmody outranked him. "All right, Gunny. If that's what you want. Who am I to argue? I just do what I'm told like a good little grunt."

"That's what I like to hear, Cherry."

"I believe that. You're not much for live and let live."

Carmody glared at him. "Don't think I'm not onto you, Cherry. I see you reading your communist propaganda. Don't think I don't."

"What propaganda?"

Carmody spit at a rock lizard. "That Chinese shit. Goddamn Chi-com mind fuck, that's all it is. Pretty soon you'll be wearing a fucking party badge and sucking Uncle Ho's dick."

Spiers almost started laughing. The book Carmody was referring to was Sun Tzu's *The Art of War,* a classic text on warfare from the Han Dynasty, written well over two thousand years ago. He found it interesting, but not so interesting he would have actually paid money for it. He never bought it, he *caught* it. The book was thrown to him from a chopper by a Green Beret on his way up to the A Shau Valley. That was six months ago and Spiers was still holding onto it. It was worn and creased and generally dog-eared, but he was always looking at it, even though he'd read it cover to cover twice. It came out of the sky, manna from heaven, so he hung onto it like a good luck charm.

"There's nothing communist about that book, Gunny."

"Shit."

He'd never believe it and Spiers knew it. Books weren't something Carmody spent much time with. He read the sports page when a newspaper made the rounds, but refused to look at the headlines because they were all written by the "pinko press." Something which Spiers found hilarious.

"That's what I like about you, Gunny. You're so fucking narrow-minded. The Pentagon pushes your buttons and you walk and talk just like a real human being."

Carmody got in close and personal. "Listen to me, Cherry. I'm not some brain dead flag-waver. I came to Vietnam to kill people. You can think it's for country and flag, but that just shows you how fucking brainwashed *you* are. I kill communists because I fucking hate 'em and I *like* killing the little fuckers. I like stepping on them the way other people like swatting flies. It gives me great fucking joy to crush the little vermin for I am one mean, heartless, motherfucking killing machine. I am the shit in Charlie's rice and every time he chews, goddamn, but he's gonna wince at my taste."

"Gunny, with all due respect, I'm beginning to think you're a first class psychopath."

"Right you are, son. I take lives, I drink blood, and fuck corpses. I make assholes pucker and balls shrink. I'm every mother's nightmare and every commander's wet dream." He grinned sardonically, dropping Spiers a wink. "Now that we've established that, let's go bag that officer."

Spiers just shrugged. He had no say in the matter and he knew it. So much for getting back to the firebase for some cold beer and a good night's sleep. They'd never be seeing FSB Deep Cut tonight. He was hopeful about tomorrow…but not very.

Carmody checked over his gear with eagerness like a teenage boy coming of age and going on his first November deer hunt, dreams of trophy bucks dancing in his head. The gleam in his eye was much the same.

"I'm taking a piss call before we go on our hike," Spiers announced.

Carmody scowled. "Figures. You got the bladder of a twelve-year-old girl. Go air your pink slit in the bushes and try not to get your skirt wet. Jesus H. Christ."

Spiers stepped behind a tree, God knows why. He'd been living in close confines with battle-scarred Marines—the crude, the rude, and the lewd—for months now and there was really nothing approaching privacy, but sometimes when you could get it, you took it…despite all the stories of the poor bastards who'd been wasted by Charlie when they slipped off to do their business.

When he got back, Carmody was staring at the fly-specked corpses broiling in the heat. "We'll be back soon," he told them. "You wait on us. Put a candle in the window."

"Let's go already," Spiers said.

Carmody grinned. It was not a pleasant sight. His teeth were like yellowed tombstones set into that seamed, painted face. "Grab your ruck, Cherry. Let's hump. We gonna bag us a Chuck and step in some shit."

But Spiers had a weird feeling they were about to step into something much worse.

Something he just couldn't put a name to.

## 2

They moved like stalking cats: quiet, controlled, predatory.

Carmody led them through the trees and it was thick brush forest, a maze of damp ferns, gnarled teak trees, snaking vines and heavy-clotted undergrowth. The ground was muddy and uneven, an obstacle course of rotting logs, fallen branches, and leafy loam four inches thick that sucked their canvas boots straight down. The triple-canopy jungle blocked out most of the light from above, creating shifting pockets of shadow and steaming rank mist. Whenever they broke free into the hot sun, it was into fields of sharp-edged razor grass that grew seven feet high and would slice exposed skin. Then it was back into the jungle again, to fight through thickets of interlocking scrub and tangled vines and muddy sinkholes while clouds of mosquitoes and gnats hovered around them in a buzzing, persistent aura.

The only good thing about any of it was that it was such primitive country—*prehistoric* is the word that passed through Spiers' mind—and so congested, that there was no way any sizeable enemy unit could move through it. So beyond small bands of VC, he didn't figure they had too much to worry about other than the local wildlife: poisonous snakes and venomous spiders and whatever other awful things that had come to term in its dripping vastness.

Carmody, who was twice his age, moved through it like an indigenous tribesmen, a fucking Nung Kit Carson scout. He did it quickly yet carefully, quietly and smoothly. He wasn't even human. He was part monkey and part snake and part mole. Nobody could move like this guy; he wasn't even human. Spiers had a hell of a time keeping up with him.

"C'mon, Marine," Carmody whispered to him, holding some fan leaves aside. "You move like my maiden aunt fucks."

And Spiers thought: *That crazy motherfucker, he's gonna lead us into a VC ambush and six months from now some ARVN grunt patrol's gonna find our bones and wonder who the hell we were.*

The countryside was a mutiny of dense vegetation and there were just too many places for the enemy to hide. And that officer…well, he could've crawled off and died just about anywhere. They could have walked within four feet of his body and never even seen him. This was bullshit. The way things were going it would be dark before they evaded to the LZ.

They crossed a spreading boggy pool of emerald green water, the surface slicked with algae and covered with gliding bugs. The bottom was slippery with flat, mossy stones and it was quite a job to keep from going on their asses with all the equipment they were carrying.

At least it was for Spiers.

Carmody moved through it like a kid, sure-footed with impeccable balance. On the other side, some fifteen feet in front of Spiers, Carmody held up a hand and Spiers stopped. His heart was thudding and he was up to his knees in the muck. If they made contact with the enemy now, he was a dead man. After a moment, Carmody motioned him forward.

"See it?" he said.

Spiers did. On a flat-bladed leaf, there were a few drops of blood.

Beyond, there was a neat little trail of it through the fronds. Many of the stems were broken, petals flipped up with the lighter undersides showing. A rotted log had been disturbed by a boot, the darker wood gouged free. Someone had been through here, someone in a hurry. Someone stumbling blindly through the brush with no attempt made to cover their progress.

It was the sort of trail an injured, desperate man might leave behind.

Carmody grinned like a viper, moving forward in a slow, careful duckwalk, eyes wide, ears open, and nose sniffing like a Bluetick hound hot on the trail of a possum. He not only saw the blood, Spiers knew, but he smelled it and nothing would stop him now. He was relentless when he was on the trail of the enemy, absolutely relentless. He was a brutal and vicious killer when he was hot on the spoor of a communist. There was no way he would stop until he greased that officer, just no way. The idea of it was unthinkable to him. It was like having sex without an orgasm and

Spiers figured for guys like Carmody that comparison was pretty damn apt.

## 3

Carmody was getting excited.

You wouldn't have known it by looking at him, but inside he could barely contain himself because he was closing in on his prey and he knew it. There was not only a science to the hunting of a man, but to reading the blood trail itself. When they'd first started out after the officer, whenever they saw a splotch of blood it was dark and dry which meant it wasn't recent. But the closer they got—and, hot damn, they were getting close—the more it began to become not old, sticky blood, but recent wet blood. Carmody was seeing more and more of it, which meant that the officer was bleeding good, real good, and soon enough, he would start seeing blood that was a brighter red in color, frothing with oxygen bubbles and when he saw that it would be time for the kill.

Spiers was right in thinking the VC had been hit good.

Carmody could tell that just by the blood the guy was losing and his drunken plunge through the underbrush. He was in a frantic hurry to escape because he knew he was being hunted. He was dying, most likely, but survival instinct was carrying him ever forward like a wounded animal. He would not stop until he lost too much blood and weakened or until things reached the point of no return and, like an animal, he crawled off somewhere to die in relative peace.

That's what bothered Carmody more than anything else, the possibility that the officer—*his* kill, as far as he was concerned—would die before he got to him. That would have been extremely disappointing for a guy like Carmody who liked his adversaries to know not only that they were being killed but by *whom.*

As he tracked through the underbrush, hunting spots of red, he saw no sign that the VC had stopped to dress his wounds. Maybe he did it while he was moving. That was a possibility. Some of those little bastards were tough SOBs. But the fact that Carmody saw no indication of any hesitation in the officer's flight made him think there was plenty of life left in him and that made him smile.

*You little zipperhead, you're giving me the most fun I've had in weeks.*

And it was fun, but it was also business. And in business you had to be hardnosed and practical. Carmody was feeling tense inside but it was a good kind of tense mixed with excitement, but he knew he had to keep the latter on a low simmer so he didn't make any mistakes. This gook officer was just like any other soldier. If he knew he was dying, he might just decide that he didn't want to die alone, that he was going to take his hunter with him. The last thing Carmody wanted to do was to stumble into a killzone and get stitched crotch to throat by an AK-47.

So he moved calmly and carefully, senses heightened.

He could hear Spiers behind him. He wasn't making too much noise, but definitely more noise than Carmody liked. Spiers was a good kid. Carmody was going to mold him into a good Marine one way or another. He was going to make a first class scout/sniper out of him whether he liked it or not. And right then, Carmody knew, he was not liking it.

Not in the least.

He was a product of his generation and the war itself. These new guys wanted to go out, make contact, kill some VC, then get back to camp in time for supper, a good drunk, and a sloppy Viet blowjob. That's what worried Carmody about the new breed of Marine. They just did not seem to embrace the suffering like the old school. Too much technology, too many fancy toys.

Sometimes, even Carmody found himself getting used to it, acclimating himself to the easy life. In Korea, scout/snipers were out on operations for days at a time, but in Vietnam it was different. They were usually day trips. The choppers made that possible. There were very few over-nighters. Now and again, he would go out with a platoon or a company-sized element, always on the hunt for VC or NVA forward observers or scouts. It was his job to take them out and he enjoyed it. But that shit was always point-and-shoot and took no real skills, no real tactics or stealth. The commanding officer would call, *"SNIPER UP!"* and tell him who he wanted taken out. How he did it was his business, long as it got done.

That stuff was okay, but it didn't have the same feel as it did inserting into the jungle with a five-man hunter/killer team and searching out targets of opportunity or going out like he and Spiers did as sniper and scout, hunting a specific target. Those were the good ones. Carmody liked it best when it was just the two of them. Two men could inflict some serious damage but were nearly impossible to track down in heavy jungle. It was cat-and-mouse and Carmody lived for it. He was good at his job and he knew it. He didn't even want to think of how many hours he'd waited on hillsides for his target to appear, not moving, barely breathing, pissing himself so he wouldn't give away his position while bugs crawled over him and snakes slid past, unaware that he was anything more than another log.

It wasn't for everyone.

Very few had the nerves and patience for it.

Particularly Americans who just wanted to charge in and win one for the team, get back to camp so they could get drunk and cheer their victory. Carmody had been in the Marine Corps a long time and he rated a desk job. The only way he was out in the field was by pulling a lot of strings and calling in a lot of favors. Out in the boonies, he was effective; pushing papers, he was useless.

*Wait. What the hell is that?*

He saw some blood on a fern, fresh blood, but that wasn't what caught his attention. There was something else just ahead caught in the grass, a strand of something white and shiny. Tripwire? He motioned for Spiers to halt and crawled forward on his belly with his K-bar knife out to see if it was a wire for a booby trap. He edged in closer through the moist loam, feeling the water soaking through the knees of his jungle utilities. The strand wasn't connected to anything. It was just laying there.

Using the blade of the knife, he pulled it free and got it into his hands. Funny. It was sticky feeling yet silky underneath. He tried to break it, but it had incredible tensile strength. At first, he was thinking it was a strand of some kind of spider web, but it wasn't spider web. It wasn't wire either...exactly. It was sort of like plastic fishing line, very fine. He cut it with his knife, but he had to saw at it and his blade was sharp enough to slit throats. Strange stuff. It could have been some new type of wire, but if it was there was no way the Viets would be using it. Everything they had was begged, borrowed, or stolen.

He motioned Spiers forward.

"What is that shit?" Spiers asked.

"I don't know. Maybe some kind of synthetic."

Spiers held it, decided he didn't like the feel of it and dropped it in the grass.

Carmody looked up into the trees. He sensed motion. For just a second, he thought he glimpsed a shadowy form moving through the high branches, but there was nothing up there. Maybe it had been a monkey. He kept staring, watching, feeling a chill along his spine that he couldn't adequately explain. There was no way a VC could be up that high, seventy feet off the ground, yet he had the most awful feeling that he was being watched. The idea was ludicrous, of course, but it persisted and he did not like it.

Spiers was staring up there, too. "What is it, Gunny?" he whispered.

Carmody shook his head. "Nothing but my imagination."

"You sure?"

"Let's go," he told Spiers. "Our day isn't done yet."

"Figured you'd say that."

Carmody slid through a stand of green bamboo, keeping an eye out for snakes, and into the heavy jungle beyond. The vegetation was like a wall pushing in at him. He could see where the VC officer had fought his way through, the broken branches and scattered leaves, snapped stems. More so, he could smell the pungent, freshly cut odor of sap.

Though he could not adequately explain it, he had a feeling of claustrophobia that he had never experienced before. It was as if the jungle was closing in on him or working against him. It was crazy either way. Jungle was just jungle. Yet, he couldn't get past a certain eerie feeling that nothing was quite like it had been before. Something had changed or shifted. *Distorted,* was the word that passed through his mind as if he had stepped off into another world now where things weren't quite the way they had been before.

"Gunny," Spiers said. "Look."

Up in the trees high above them there were more strands of that white stuff, not only strands but sheets of it like Angel's Hair tangled up in the greenery. It was ragged, sheared looking. It seemed to float up there, moving as if it were urged by some gentle breeze or was maybe lighter than the air itself.

"Weird shit," was all Carmody would say.

"What the hell is it?" Spiers asked him.

He didn't know what it was, but he didn't like it. There was something positively unnatural about it. But he wasn't here for nature study. He had a very real job to do and he needed to concentrate 100% on that. He couldn't let anything interfere with his thought processes. He was hunting a wounded man, a dying man that had nothing left to lose and there wasn't a more dangerous animal in the world than that.

He saw a few more drops of blood.

The excitement rose in him again.

He was getting close to his quarry.

*I'm coming for you, Mr. Charlie Gook. I'm coming to get you, you fucking baby killer. You can bank on that.*

They moved over a ridge shrouded by thick bushes and down a steep hillside where the greenery was even more congested, more dense, full of vines and shoots and snaking tendrils. They took it real slow, placing their booted feet carefully and keeping an eye out for tripwires and booby traps. They found more blood at the bottom where the hill leveled into a marshy hollow filled with brown, sucking mud and giant purple-edged ferns. Black flies nipped at their necks and forearms. Snakes slid away through the muck and tiny, unseen animals skittered through the cane grass. Huge, vibrant blue butterflies drifted in the haze.

The late afternoon heat was turgid and suffocating. It lay on their skins like a sheen of hot wax, wrapped hands around their throats, flicked stinging sweat into their eyes. "Up ahead," Carmody said, pausing. "A ville, I think."

Spiers studied the village with his spotting scope.

He saw no signs of life. It looked abandoned. Still, he saw no reason to take chances. If that officer was able to hook up with a VC or NVA unit, then they might be walking into an ambush.

"I say we by-pass."

Carmody shook his head. "Negative. The blood trail leads here. My guess is our Charlie Gook is hiding in one of those hootches, bleeding out. I'll tag him, piss on his corpse, insult his mother, and we'll call it a day, Cherry."

"I don't like it."

"Sooner we bag our Chuck, the sooner we make that LZ and pop smoke and the sooner you're back at the FSB with your communist propaganda and your whores and your hippy music. Besides, I'm getting hungry. I could use some chop."

"All right. Let's get it done."

"I like the way you think, son."

4

They came out of the hollow and slipped through waist-deep elephant grass until a clearing opened up. The little hamlet sat out there in a pocket of shimmering heat waves. Just a scant collection of bamboo huts and thatched sheds. They were in bad shape: roofs collapsed, walls sagging. A few had fallen right over. Abandoned, and abandoned for some time apparently.

Spiers said, "We better stay away from there. I'm getting a funny feeling."

It was the perfect place for Charlie to set-up a little tea party replete with bullets and grenades, maybe a few mortar rounds to spice things up a bit. Be one thing going in there with a reinforced squad…but just two guys? Suicide. He could just about picture Carmody getting blown away in the first volley and himself getting taken prisoner. He didn't think he'd do real well in a jungle prison camp. Starvation and dysentery just weren't his things.

Carmody had his map and compass out, was jotting down the position of the village for future operations. Finally, he slipped them back into a zippered pocket of his jungle fatigue pants. He took his ruck off and set it in the grass, set his bolt-action Winchester sniping rifle alongside it.

He checked the action on his M-16. "I'm going in there, Cherry, to have a look. You wait here until I tell you different. If that fuck's hiding in there, I'll do him and we can get out of here. I don't come back—"

"Send in the Marines?"

Carmody smiled thinly and broke cover, moving in a loping zig-zag pattern through the grass until he found the first hut. He swung low through the doorway. Then he came out, started checking them one by one. He disappeared behind a long, low shed at the far perimeter and Spiers just waited and waited.

*Goddamn Carmody,* he was thinking, *sonofabitch has been in the Corps thirty years, is pushing fifty, and look at him out there. He moves like he's twenty, hell, like he's twelve. He's good. Ain't nobody better.*

And Spiers wondered if he was thinking these things because they were true or because he wanted to convince himself that Carmody was too damn slick for any gook to grease. He figured it was both.

At a casual pace, Carmody came back. "Clear," he said. He shouldered his pack and rifle, wiped sweat from the ruts under his eyes. "I found some blood. He came through here, all right. Found something else, too."

Beyond the hootch at the far side is where Carmody took him, to the fringe of the jungle. Spiers didn't see anything but a solid wall of vines and creepers that hung from the trees overhead. Then Carmody parted them and he saw all right.

But what?

He wasn't sure. Some shrunken thing with gray, flaking skin like tree bark and a face that was more skull than flesh. Like dirty papier-mâché plastered tightly to jutting bone beneath. The mummy had its hands tied behind its back. Its body was impaled on a stake shoved in its crotch. It had to be real old, all gone to leather like that. He was thinking maybe it was some old woman, some bag of bones like an old hag-witch in a storybook.

"Why the hell would they do this to some old Viet?" he said to Carmody, brushing a leaf spider from his knee. "Looks like they dug her up, stuck her on this pole. Crazy bastards."

Carmody just shook his head, staring at that death mask, seeing the black holes for eyes and discolored teeth like fence posts set in black, puckered earth. "It ain't no woman, Cherry. And it ain't no Viet." He touched the corded flesh at the cadaver's neck, pulled off what looked like a necklace. But it wasn't a necklace. "Dog tags," he said.

Disgusted, offended, Spiers took them from him and they were black with something. He scraped at the upraised letters and numbers with his thumbnail. "John...John Cohen. U.S. Army...oh for fuck's sake, Gunny. Gotta be a joke...that ain't no American soldier."

But Carmody just shrugged. "Was once."

Spiers just stood there, the hot air swimming around him like ectoplasm. Beads of sweat ran down his face, dripping from his chin. He opened his mouth to protest, to argue the fact...then closed it again. All right, all right, if that guy was a soldier, then what in the hell had happened to him? He looked like something that fell from a spider's web.

Spiers didn't like any of this.

He'd had a bad feeling from the start that had steadily been growing worse and now it was like a black mass settling into the pit of his belly. He looked around the deserted village, wondering why it had been emptied and maybe by *what*. The mummified corpse was like a scarecrow left there to warn them off.

He sighed, not sure what to think. He put the tags in his shirt pocket. Command would want them. One more MIA accounted for. *John Cohen.* Standing there, he wondered what John Cohen's life had been like before the war. Who had he been and what? What were his plans for the future and what the hell was he doing out this far? In his mind, he pictured Cohen as a sandy-haired, freckle-faced kid playing sandlot baseball. He would never have thought that ten or fifteen years later he'd be a particularly ugly scarecrow with a stake shoved up its ass in some deserted village in Southeast Asia.

"This isn't right," Spiers said.

"Ain't nothing right in this war, son."

But Carmody wasn't getting it. It had wings and it flew right over the top of his pointy head or, at the very least, he wanted to give that impression. Spiers was disturbed by the mummy in too many ways. Was Cohen dead when the Viets put him on that stake? Just some KIA they impaled as a sick joke? Or had he been alive and screaming? And what was the point? A warning? A slap in the face? Or was it something much darker that was beyond comprehension?

"He's been dead a long time, son. Ain't nothing you can do for him," Carmody said.

Spiers nodded and turned away from the body. "Let's get the hell out of here, Gunny."

## 5

Back into the sweltering confines of the jungle.

It was an envelope of screaming white noise—chattering monkeys, shrilling birds, croaking frogs, singing insects, a thousand other busy, living sounds. That was the soundtrack of the rain forest. A seething, multi-hued, overcrowded zoo of life forms competing to stay alive just one more day.

Monsoon season had just ended and the ground was a series of muddy pools and bubbling streams and ankle-deep muck. Each time Spiers put a boot down, clouds of gnats rose into the air. The countryside was little better than a bog. It was wet and spongy and full of huge leeches. He knew from experience that if you slogged through the watery mud for very long, boots and socks had a tendency to become saturated and fall apart. At Phu Loc, they'd waded through shit like this day after day after day hunting an NVA command post and what they got for their troubles were men down with snakebite and exhaustion, their feet infected with immersion foot and jungle rot. The medics had to cut the boots off some of the grunts and their feet were white and swollen, split open with sores.

But that was 'Nam, he knew.

Half the fight was with the VC and NVA, the other half was with the elements. The baking heat of the dry season and the sucking mud of the monsoons. All the standing water created favorable breeding conditions for immense swarms of mosquitoes that descended on you in dark, buzzing clouds, feasting on your blood. You had to breathe through clenched teeth so you didn't inhale them. Even so, you were constantly digging them out of your nostrils and ears, spitting them out of your mouth. A Montagnard Kit Carson scout had once told him that in the remote villages in the Highlands there were swarms of mosquitoes so dense that they would turn the sky black. When that happened, the villagers would get under cover. He said he had found the remains of goats that were tied to trees that had been drained completely dry.

Whether that was true or not, he didn't know, but he had seen dozens of men down with malaria from mosquito bites. It was a nasty disease of chills, fevers, vomiting, diarrhea, and eventually death if left untreated. It had reached epidemic proportions in Indochina and thousands died every year from it.

Carmody paused atop a ridgeline, in a drooping thicket of stunted, wind-blasted trees. He made more notations on his map and consulted his compass continually. That's how Spiers knew they were inside Cambodia—he was doing it all the time, scribbling things down. Spiers had suspected it for some time, but there was no real way to know. The Viets and Cambodes were real vague on borders. They tended to change with the seasons. Borders were more the province of western mapmakers, particularly when you were talking hilly, jungled slopes like this. What difference did it really make?

Spiers squatted down by Carmody. "So how long we been in Cambodia, Gunny?"

"About an hour," he said, staring off into the forest. "Give or take."

It was illegal as hell, but it wasn't like it hadn't been done before by small spec ops and LRRP teams. Everyone knew that just as they knew the North Vietnamese used Cambodia as a staging area. They operated huge bases there, stockpiling men and supplies and weapons for across the border operations into Vietnam where they hit American units, sneaking back to hide and lick their wounds. The U.S. wasn't allowed to wage war in Cambodia. The Cambodians were a sovereign nation claiming neutrality between Hanoi and Washington. The truth was, they just looked the other way so as not to stir up trouble. The North Vietnamese had said again and again that they did not operate bases in Cambodia, but that was a bald-faced lie. Sooner or later, Spiers figured, Washington was going to give the okay and the NVA strongholds were going to be shattered. But until then, it was all a matter of fucking politics.

And that was the problem with the whole damn war: too many rules for the U.S. and none for the North Viets.

"You know something," Carmody said as they paused. "I'm starting to think that this gook has made one hell of a run for a dying man."

"Maybe he's not dying at all."

"Gotta be. He's lost a lot of blood." Carmody shook his head. "He must be one tough SOB."

"One tough SOB that might be drawing us into a pissing contest with an NVA company."

"Maybe."

"Then let's evade out of here before things get hairy."

"They're already hairy. That's why we got to tag this Victor Charlie. If he's making this kind of run, I have to think he's got something on his person he don't want us to get our hands on."

But that was a trap. Nine times out of ten, Spiers knew, these guys had nothing of value on them. And it wasn't unusual for the VC and NVA to plant bullshit documents on their officers to waste American time. They were nothing if not crafty. That was the only way they kept their head above water in a punch-up with the world's most technologically advanced, best trained, and best supplied army. If Carmody was going after this guy for what he *might* be carrying, this whole thing was a fucking waste of time.

"I'll give him another mile, but no more."

Spiers just shrugged. "All right. I'm holding you to that."

"I'm willing to bet you are."

They tracked for another fifteen or twenty minutes and then Carmody found more blood from their quarry who seemed to have an endless supply of the stuff. *Fucking guy's like a sprinkling can,* Spiers thought. He decided that Carmody's hard-on for this guy was more than just what he might be carrying or who he was trying to link up with. This Viet was one tough sonofabitch and Carmody respected that—if he was a VC he would have been this guy. He probably wanted to meet him and shake his hand, right before he killed him.

They paused at the edge of a brown, slow-moving creek. "Okay, Cherry. I'm getting a good blood trail now. You wait here. I'm going to go grease that little shit. I'm not back in thirty minutes, you do not come to get me, understand?"

"Sure, Gunny."

"You proceed back into Vietnam and get yourself to the LZ and wait for extraction. No hero shit. You do not come after me."

With that, Carmody took off and Spiers waited. It was all bullshit. Marines didn't leave other Marines behind. If he didn't come back, Spiers would have to go after him. It was how things worked. Waiting there, he planned out how he would get back across the border carrying a wounded man or a corpse.

6

During the siege of Khe Sanh in '68, Carmody got on the wrong end of a 60mm Chicom mortar. He was manning a .50 cal when the shell came burning down into their sector and so close it killed two Marines and injured three others. He was one of them. He took shrapnel to his left arm. So much of it, he joked later, that when he moved his fucking arm it rattled. And it was too bad because things were just getting good.

The saturation bombing of the surrounding hills where the NVA were dug in was reaching its height of destruction.

There wasn't a Marine there that wasn't digging it. After months and months of non-stop harassment and shelling by the numerically superior NVA force beyond the wire, this was payback. Those ugly, battle-scarred hills were being pulverized and flattened. And what a wonderful thing that was. Air Force, Marine, and Navy pilots flew one sortie after another raining down missiles and napalm, defoliants and 750-pound bombs, blowing Charlie's hiding places into so much debris and mulch. After many months of humping those hills and crawling through them on night patrol, getting ambushed and blown to shit on their winding trails and losing limbs and life in their twisted shadows, here was payback, here was scorched earth, here was an NVA nightmare in the flesh. They said 110,000 tons of bombs were dropped and when it was done, you could believe it because the big hills were gutted with craters and the small ones no longer existed. The NVA trench lines and bunkers were turned inside out and upside down. The countryside was pitted and plucked like the flesh of a leper, a jagged run of sores and contusions and deep, gaping holes. Who could say how many thousands of the enemy had been blasted, blown to bits, burned, and buried alive?

Carmody was sent to a hospital in Da Nang where the surgeons removed the shrapnel from his arm. He was lucky, no nerve damage or torn ligaments. He stayed there for a month knitting up, his arm in a cast, which was about as boring as boring got, especially for a guy who was used to being in the field pissing off the enemy. His third week there, there had been some heavy fighting up along the DMZ and the wounded were coming in quite regularly. The bad ones went down to Saigon and off to Hawaii. At Da Nang, they removed bullets and shrapnel, fought infection and removed limbs when there was no other way.

About three days into his stay, Carmody woke up in the middle of the night and looked around the crowded ward, wondering why the hell they were wasting a bed on him when there were real casualties. That's when he noticed something that left him cold.

There was a VC on the ward.

A fucking gook in black pajamas was laying not two beds away, his head and arm bandaged up, some kind of tube coming out of his chest. Carmody was beside himself. This was one of the little shitters that was filling up the wards with wounded and they were *treating* him? What the fuck was this war coming to?

When one of the nurses came through, Carmody said, "What is that fucking slope doing in an American hospital?"

The nurse shrugged and told him that intelligence wanted this particular one. They wanted him patched up and stabilized so he could be interrogated. The nurse didn't look like she liked it either, but orders were orders. There were two MPs assigned to watch over him, but they spent most of their time out in the corridor flirting with the nurses.

That's when Carmody figured the VC was his responsibility.

Most of the soldiers on the ward weren't even conscious. Many would never regain consciousness again because of that little bastard in their midst. He just couldn't imagine what they were going to think if they woke up and saw that puke. It would take more than a couple pussy-happy MPs to keep them off him, regardless of their condition. The only thing that gave him pleasure was what the VC was going to think when he woke up with all the Americans around him. He'd be scared shitless, of course. Not just because of where he was but because he would know he was only being kept alive so he could be questioned, something he ultimately wouldn't survive.

Carmody kept his eye on him.

He remembered hearing once how a VC like this guy, all shot to hell, was in a hospital and he still had enough strength to get up, break a bottle and slit the throat of a wounded Australian soldier.

*Well, that ain't going to fucking happen here.*

The insane thing was, it almost did. Carmody dozed off and opened his eyes, sensing movement. The VC was up out of bed, rummaging around. He found a pair of scissors and he was planning on doing some damage before he joined that asshole Ho Chi Minh in the afterlife. He didn't count on Carmody. He turned around and there was a big Marine standing behind him.

He cried out and tried to stab Carmody with the scissors. Carmody blocked the blow and the scissors lodged in his cast. By the time they did, he had hit the VC so hard in the chest with an open palm blow that he clearly heard his sternum crack. The VC dropped to his knees. Carmody yanked out his chest tube and proceeded to stomp his head until he lost consciousness. By the time the MPs arrived, the little bastard was dead.

"What the hell happened here?" one of the MPs asked.

"He fell out of bed," Carmody told him.

There was some trouble over that and intelligence was pissed off, but all they could get out of Carmody was that he'd been sent to Vietnam to kill communists and this little fucker had gone after him with scissors, so he reacted in kind.

He was reminded of that whole episode as he tracked the officer because like that VC in the hospital, this guy just would not die easily. He was just as determined and the more determined he became to stay alive, the more determined Carmody was to kill him. It was more than a battle of ideologies here, more than enemy against enemy, it was a battle of wills and Carmody had every confidence that, in the end, he would be victorious because for a guy like him, there was no such thing as failure.

# 7

About twenty minutes after Carmody went out hunting, he came back. "I think I know where he went," he said.

Spiers just looked at him. This was all getting absurd. He was all for letting the little pricker live, but Carmody was hot on the scent and there was no way he'd turn back now. And, as Carmody liked to point out again and again, every dead Viet meant an alive American and you couldn't argue with the logic of that.

"Let's go," Carmody said.

"I'm with you."

But he wasn't going fast enough because Carmody snarled, "Move your ass, Cherry! *Di di mau, motherfucker!*"

Carmody led off and Spiers followed him.

Up hills and down vales, slogging through swamps and fern-filled hollows. Carmody kept finding his blood spoor and Spiers was picking off leeches and starting to think that VC officer was superhuman, making it this far with a torn-open belly. Finally, a wide valley opened before them, like a deep bowl scooped from the earth and filled with a lush, shimmering green. It went on so far, it faded into a hazy mist at the horizon.

What Spiers didn't like about it right away was the complete absence of any trails or roads down there. And from this height, looking down into the valley, he should've been able to see them—parts of them—if they were there. But all he saw was thick, impenetrable jungle, primordial and timeless. Pockets of mist hung in the trees. It was like something straight out of the Jurassic. Virgin territory, unexplored, untenanted by man.

"Down there?" he said.

Carmody nodded. "That's where he went."

"This valley got a name?"

But Carmody just shook his head, licked his lips. "No. Not even on the map. Course…lot of things aren't on this map. I already sketched in a river, two swamps, and about a dozen big hills not on here."

Spiers kept staring down there and something in him, some indefinable thing, had woken up and did not like what it saw. It was telling him that now was a good time to turn back, because nothing good could come of going down there. And if he had to put a finger on it, he would've said it was fear. Dread. A raw, inexplicable terror like standing before a haunted house on a dare, knowing you should turn back, but realizing you couldn't.

"This is bullshit, Gunny. We better get back."

"Shit, we almost got him, Cherry."

Spiers shook his head. "Gunny, ain't no way a gut-shot man made it this far."

Carmody explained to him that he probably *wasn't* gut-shot. It had just looked like it in the scope. The slug probably got deflected off a rib, didn't really tear up his bowels at all. "Seen it happen. Wound like that? Guy can go all day before he drops. Bleeds a lot, but that's about it."

But Spiers still didn't like it. His military training and experience were telling him that this valley was a good place to stash an NVA base camp or a VC battalion hospital, both of which would be heavily fortified. He told Carmody the same. "You know how those little fucks are. If they could tunnel into a turd, they'd hang curtains on the windows."

"True. Very true. What I'm seeing here is the perfect place to run ops over the border," Carmody said. "If that's the case, we better have a look."

"Jesus Christ, Gunny."

"Do it for honor and country, son. And if you don't buy my propaganda and flag-waving, then do it because I told you to and I'm in command of this here sight-seeing tour."

Spiers still didn't like it.

They hadn't seen so much as a sign of human habitation in many, many miles. They were really out in the boonies here. So far out that there weren't even any peasant hootches or any indication of indigenous peoples. This was just too far for the NVA or VC to use. It wouldn't have been practical. It would have taken many days to walk to the nearest U.S. installation or to even bump into a stray patrol. No, there was nothing down there and he knew it. At least, nothing he'd want to meet.

"I think we should reconsider," he said.
"Objection overruled," Carmody told him.

8

Down they went, clawing over fallen trees and rocky outcroppings, squeezing between volcanic crevices, fighting all the way through thick and moist vegetation that climbed over their heads and plunged them into a rank, silent darkness just as hot as the inside of a leather bag. The trees were covered with moss and the ground was muddy, set with potholes and sudden dips anxious to snap an ankle.

This was virgin territory, primeval rain forest untenanted by man. There were immense stands of bamboo, gnarled mahogany, teak, and ebony trees that rose two hundred feet above creating a dense canopy of interlocking branches and tangled vines. The valley floor was swampy and brush-covered, gigantic ferns and multi-colored orchids rising up in a dizzying array. Spiers was beside himself. There were spreading, fetid pools of leeches and clouds of mosquitoes, unseen things hopping and slithering in the flooded vegetation. Lizards leapt on rotting logs. Huge chittering bats hung upside down in the trees. He saw hairy brown spiders bigger than his hand and centipedes longer than his forearm. Ticks the size of quarters crawled over his boots.

As they moved forward, he kept an eye out for deadly bamboo vipers, kraits, and king cobras that liked to hunt rodents in the underbrush. He saw none, but he did see a gigantic Burmese python hanging in a tree that had to be well over twenty feet long.

In a little clearing flanked by crowded stands of twisted bamboo, they found four more cadavers impaled on stakes. They were shriveled like the other one, skeletons wrapped tight in dirty, corrugated flesh. Skull faces mopped with stringy black hair, strands of it hanging over black eye sockets. Jaws sprung and screaming. Asians, though, not Americans.

"Gunny…I don't like this," Spiers said, the fear bubbling beneath his words like lava. "This…I don't know…it's like a warning or something."

But Carmody didn't want to hear it.

They pushed their way into the bamboo and the heat was stifling. In about ten minutes, they broke through and climbed a low hill, pausing while Carmody jotted on his map again. Spiers sat on a rock, vines set with brilliant orange blossoms trailing all around him.

Something was wrong, but he didn't know what.

He had a crazy, incontrovertible feeling they were not alone, that they were being watched. That eyes were all around them, waiting and studying. His throat was parched and swigging from his canteen did nothing to relieve it. Below them, to either side, that black enclosing jungle was completely, utterly silent, as if it was holding its breath.

They heard a sound.

A stumbling, crashing noise.

Carmody had his spotting scope out. "There he is, Cherry. There's our boy." He was excited...yet, *concerned.* He handed Spiers the scope while he unpacked his modified Winchester Model 70. "Keep an eye on him."

Spiers found the officer, saw him stumble through the undergrowth below them and into a meadow of knee-high ferns. He was covered with blood, looked to be in pain. He started first this way, paused, moved in the other direction, stopped. Turned in circles. Maybe he was feverish, hallucinating. It looked like he was lost or...*terrified.*

And that's what Spiers was thinking: *Look at him—he's scared like a spooked rabbit. He don't know which way to move. I don't know what he's afraid of, but I bet it isn't us—*

At that moment, there was a sound that cut through the still air like a shrilling air raid siren, except this was low and droning and reminded him of somebody blowing over the top of an empty bottle. It had that same ghostly caliber, but it was loud and cycling, rising and falling and then fading out altogether. It was the most singularly eerie and unearthly noise he had ever heard.

Both he and Carmody were pressed together tightly after that.

They stood there, shaking, waiting for it to come again but it didn't. Spiers' mouth was so dry he couldn't even manage a whisper to ask what it might have been. His imagination was working overtime. There was no way it could have been an animal, not with that kind of volume. Whatever it was, it had been not only unnatural but on purpose. His whirling brain could not think of what that purpose might be, but it sure as hell was no accident.

"Let's get that Charlie Gook," Carmody said in a quiet, weak voice. "Fuck the rest of this."

Spiers had him on the scope again as Carmody brought up his rifle.

The VC kept moving in circles, starting into the jungle, then shambling back away from it. He looked at the ground, into the forest, up into the trees. He was like some cornered animal, afraid, trapped, knowing death was coming, but not from where or what form it would take.

*Jesus H. Christ.*

Spiers went right over on his ass, making a weird choking sound in his throat, trying to suck wind that suddenly wasn't there. Carmody was shaking him and shaking him. *"What is it, Cherry? What the hell is it?"*

But Spiers wasn't sure.

He'd been looking at the Viet down there running around in circles and then…and then there'd been a weird blurring motion coming from above and something long and white and writhing had whipped out of nowhere, snatched that sonofabitch up into the air. Right up into the air and fast, unbelievably fast.

"Goddammit, Cherry!" Carmody said in a hard, grating whisper. "He got away! What the fuck is wrong with you?"

But Spiers wasn't sure. He tried to speak, but his voice was lodged down deep in his throat and he couldn't get it out.

"Spiers! Goddammit, Marine, you answer me!"

"He…he was there…and then he was gone," he said in a high, squeaking voice. "Something…something came out of the trees…came out of the trees and grabbed him…"

But Carmody didn't want to hear that and told him to start making some sense. "Get on your feet, goddammit! Move! Right fucking now, Cherry! Or I swear to God I'll leave your worthless ass out here!"

He meant it. Spiers knew he meant it. Master Gunnery Sergeant Ronald J. Carmody did not fuck around. He was as incapable of it as he was of feeling sympathetic towards the enemy and particularly, goddamn communists. Still, Spiers did not move. Even the mighty wrath of Carmody could not shake the fear of what he had seen. Not that Carmody was accepting of that. "You sonofabitch," he said, giving Spiers a kick in the ribs that bowled him over and then another in the ass that drove him face-first into the moist loam of the valley which smelled, amazingly, much like the rich black soil of Boone County, Missouri where he was born and raised. "The time I invested in you! The goddamn time I wasted making you into a man, into a fucking Marine only to have you fold-up on me and play pussy when I need you the most!" Carmody aimed two more kicks at him, each one landing harder than the one before. "You're not taking anything I'm not! I'm crawling through the fucking shit with you! I'm in the mud and the heat! I got leeches crawling on me and bugs in my ears and fever in my brain!" His voice was rising with his anger now and his face was like some evil, leering tribal mask of a demon. "WHO THE FUCK DO YOU THINK YOU ARE TO FUCKING FOLD UP ON ME, YOU YELLOW COCKSUCKING MAGGOT? HOW FUCKING DARE YOU INSULT ME AND MY ESTEEMED MARINE CORPS BY GIVING UP AND BENDING OVER AND SHOWING THE ENEMY THE MOIST HAIRY SLIT BETWEEN YOUR FUCKING LEGS! *YOU MOTHERFUCKER! YOU WORTHLESS SACK OF MONKEY SHIT! YOU GUTLESS COWARDLY FAGGOT MAMA'S BOY SQUIRT OF FUCKING PIG PISS!"*

Automatically, his brain conditioned by months of rigorous training, Spiers got to his feet. His rifle was clutched tightly in white-knuckled fists. Carmody slapped him across the face. "Don't you dare fucking disappoint me again, goddamn you," he said. Spiers was in step again, his head screwed on tight, and his balls down below where they belonged and not lodged in the back of his throat. He moved silently behind Carmody until they reached the meadow and Carmody was sniffing around, prodding every bush and creeper with the barrel of his Winchester.

There was a smell in the air—not the hot jungle or the decaying undergrowth. Something worse, a raw and savage stink. Like blood. Like something moldering and rancid, a huge and vaporous odor.

Spiers was staring up into the trees.

Triple-canopied jungle overhead, the trees growing into one another in a thick, spreading mass of tangled and bunched foliage. An impenetrable wall of green through which scant, misty fingers of sunlight knifed. A battalion could have hid up there.

Or something much worse.

There was movement above, very high above. A few sticks fell, bouncing off tree limbs all the way down. They both saw that one of them was glistening with blood, fresh blood.

Spiers' eyes were glassy and unblinking, cords standing out in his throat. His mouth was forming words he was not even aware of. A creeping chill ran up his spine and something in him had seized up again.

"Where is he, Cherry?" Carmody was asking.

"He's up there, Gunny," Spiers said with perfect clarity. "Something took him up into the trees. Something white. It grabbed him...and yanked him up into the trees."

Maybe Carmody wanted to slap him, yell at him, abuse him again, but he didn't. For he seemed to sense it, too, that awful alien sensation of being scrutinized, watched. He stared up there and a few leaves drifted down.

"Let's go," he said, pushing Spiers towards the hill.

Then they were moving and Spiers wasn't able to get on track again, because he could feel it, whatever it was, following them from above, closing in on them. Carmody led them away quickly, through muddy pools and broad-leafed ferns, through groves of bamboo and tight thickets of scrub brush. Overhead, they could hear sounds from time to time—rustling sounds that kept an easy, effortless pace with them. And the smell of death was everywhere—like meat and blood and putrescence.

Carmody drew them into a copse of soft green jungle.

He crouched there, studied all directions, wondering, wondering. "You ever been hunted, Cherry?"

But Spiers just crouched there by him, his mouth slack, his eyes big and empty.

"I have. Up near the DMZ. Me and this gook sniper hunted each other for three days through the jungle. I finally popped that prick in a river cut—right in the temple." His eyes grew misty, haunted at the memory of those days and nights when death hunted death. "I remember how it felt—the way a deer must feel or a rabbit. And I feel like that right now."

Spiers was feeling it, too.

He'd been in a lot of tight spots in the war, times when he was inches from death, the rounds flying and Russian-made rockets tearing up great hunks of real estate and men were dying, splashing him with blood in their death throes. He'd once been out with a Marine hunter/killer team, five grunts, at Hai Van Pass, and they'd fought it tooth and nail throughout the night with a company-sized NVA unit, calling in fire missions, walking artillery shells around their perimeter and listening to the NVA soldiers scream in the blackness as they wormed in the grass, dismembered and maimed. He'd been scared to death but he didn't fold up. This was different. It was one thing to be hunted by men; that was the nature of warfare. This was something else. He had never felt so absolutely vulnerable before, his heart pounding, lungs gasping, and blood rushing. He was more than the enemy, he was prey. He was more than scared, he was oddly...*exhilarated.* As if everything inside him was pumping frantically to keep him alive, reaching out that much farther, trying to give him an edge so that he might stay alive.

Carmody decided to walk slack while Spiers led them out. They were near the edge of the valley now, a few jungled slopes, tree-covered hills, and spreading bogs and they could climb out. They'd be out of the hunting grounds. They'd be safe, they'd be free of whatever godless horror was stalking them with what seemed relentless precision.

Carmody told him he wanted to be in back, because that's where it was coming from. Whatever it was. It was coming from behind them.

Spiers humped it up one hill and down another, slogging through pools of green-slicked water, and squeezing through congested stands of sap-smelling bamboo, breaking through immense spider webs with the barrel of his rifle. He stopped from time to time, listening, watching, then moving on. He wanted to run, but his training simply would not allow anything that reckless.

*Not far now, not too far. Another fifteen minutes and you can start climbing out of this pit and into the world above.*

But already the shadows were growing long, they were clustering and spreading, leaning out at him like knife blades. Each pocket of darkness seemed to be filled with threat. He kept going, fighting to get free of the valley.

Carmody suddenly grabbed Spiers' shoulder, stopping him dead. He froze up from toes to scalp, looking, listening, waiting.

"What?" he finally said.

"Quiet."

Spiers looked around, waiting for it. The shadows continued to lengthen, a ground mist rising up out of the thick, bunched vegetation. He could hear the hammering of his own heart in his ears, but nothing else. Then—yes, a crackling sound overhead as if something big was picking its way through the branches at them, trying to get above them so it could drop on them. The sound was far off to the left, then it moved above and in front of them, then off to the right. Now it was behind them. It was like whatever was up in the trees was circling them as if maybe it wasn't quite sure where they were.

Sweat ran down the back of his neck and dripped off the tip of his nose. He had a mad desire to start busting rounds, to put out massive fire into the branches above. The sounds were still circling, but cutting in closer to their position with every turn. He was sure that any moment now something shaggy and slavering would drop from above.

But nothing did.

*It* was up there, but *it* was not ready to show itself. And maybe that was part of the game, ratcheting up the fear of its prey until they panicked and bolted as any hunted animal would do in a burst of necessary terror-driven catharsis.

Carmody kept watch with him, but unlike other times in the jungle they did not know what they were watching *for*. Dinks in black pajamas brandishing Russian rifles and Chinese grenades seemed positively pedestrian. This was bigger, this was fucking colossal.

Carmody opened his mouth, probably to tell Spiers to move out, but his jaw snapped shut like a trapdoor straining on its spring because another sound cut through the primeval green world of the valley: this one was high-pitched and screeching and it came in short bursts like locusts calling out from a stripped field of barley. It came and went, but it echoed in their heads with volume: *sssskrrreeeeek!* Each time it shrilled, it was like a fork had been dragged up their spines. Their ears rang with it and their hearts skipped beats.

And the worst thing, the very worst thing, was that it seemed to be *answered.* Each time it cut through the air, dozens of other like sounds echoed from the secret depths of the forest.

When it was quiet for maybe five minutes, Carmody said, "You lead us out, son." He put a hand on Spiers' shoulder and gave it a fatherly squeeze. "Regardless of what happens, you keep going. You do not stop. You do not come back for me. Do you understand?"

Spiers nodded.

"Now hump it, Marine!"

Then they were on the move again. There were a few hairy moments when Spiers thought his internal guidance system, so finely tuned at Scout/Sniper School, had abandoned him and he was leading them deeper into the depths of that crawling green hell. But then he broke free of the heaviest jungle and to the rising wall of the valley.

He led on, climbing up through the knotted vegetation, eyes forward, always forward, something telling him they would be safe if they could just get up and out of there. He could hear Carmody picking his way behind him and suddenly that smell—that horrible, nearly primitive odor—assailed his nostrils and got down into his belly with fingers of cold nausea. It started to grow stronger and stronger, a threatening, boiling miasma. It wasn't the stink of death. Not exactly. This was a dark sweetness that was cloying, pungent and gagging.

And he heard Carmody, below and behind him, say, "That stink…oh my Christ, that stink…"

But Spiers kept moving, kept fighting and pulling himself up and up, using gnarled tree roots and greasy vines to get himself out of there. By then, they'd been climbing for twenty minutes or more. He heard a strange, sweeping motion behind him and a muffled grunt. But it was just Carmody clawing his way up, that's all it was. And Spiers, frantic now, his heart hammering, kept going until he realized there were no sounds at all behind him, just a pall of shifting silence.

He turned around.

Carmody was gone.

Gone…just gone.

Wiping sweat from his eyes, Spiers looked in every possible direction. Up in the trees he sensed a stealthy, sentient motion.

Sucking in hot wind, he cried out: "GUNNY! GUNNY! GUNNY!"

His voice echoed out through the valley, coming back at him from a dozen locations and finally breaking up all around him. And in the trees above there was a stealthy rustling. More leaves fell. A branch tumbled earthward. And he heard an awful, hideous rending sound like meat being pulled from bone.

And then he was scrambling away and as he climbed that final lip out of the foliage, he heard a huge and resounding roar like that of some primal beast reverberate through the valley. An angry, cheated sound.

And then he was free.

Free and running as the sun set, casting a black pall over the land.

# 9

Night.

The rain was coming down and the jungle had gone to marsh and Spiers was more dead than alive, still running, charging through the bush and slogging through the mud. He'd lost his pack and his sniper rifle—and Christ, the lieutenant, tight-assed butter bar bastard was gonna be pissed about that—but he still had his M-16, but he was low on ammo. Only half a magazine left if that because once he broke free of the valley, he just lost it. The glue that held him together dried up and blew away and he panicked, started capping rounds at shadows and trees and clumps of brush. He burned three mags like that and later, when he had time to think about it and what a dumbassed cherry he was, he could not even remember doing it.

In his head, the entire time during that mad flight, was his voice: *Gonna get out of here, gonna reach that LZ and pop smoke and wait for the bird, gonna get back to Saigon and grab a plane back home, eat the apple and fuck the war and fuck the Corps.*

He was lost, wet, and filthy and he couldn't seem to get his bearings. He was honestly afraid to stop and try. Because if he stopped, that thing might catch up with him. He didn't know what it was, but his scarred soul told him it was a man-eater, it was a monster, it was some gigantic and hungry thing that picked its teeth with the bones of men.

Finally, exhausted, drenched with rain and sweat, leeches hanging off him like remoras on a shark's belly, he stopped. In fact, he collapsed. The world went funny and his head spun and his knees locked up and he dropped into the mud, panting, gasping, whimpering under his own breath. He had to get his shit together. His Marine discipline and his scout training demanded it. If he couldn't figure out where he was and get a fix, he'd never find that LZ. He'd die out here and animals would pick his carcass down to white bones.

*Think, man, you got to fucking think! You're making enough noise to draw every fucking gook for miles! Think now, think!*

But his brain seemed incapable of it. It was the machine that stopped, a seized gear, a cog ground to a halt. Up to his hips in that black, slow-sluicing mud, he could only breathe and wish to God he'd never heard of the fucking Marine Corps and Viet-fucking-nam.

He pulled himself up, shouldering his rifle, and staggered beneath a tree to get out of the rain. He unzipped one of the pockets in his jungle fatigues and pulled out the plastic baggie he kept his cigarettes and lighter in. Still dry. Thank God, still dry. Cupping his hands for light suppression the way he'd been trained, he pulled off his cigarette and the nicotine helped. His head began to clear and he was able to think, to recall what had happened. But it was crazy. It was fucking *dinky dau* crazy.

"Gunny," he said under his breath, feeling like he'd just lost his father. "Gunny."

He had abandoned him back there. That's what his guilt told him. But it wasn't true, it just wasn't fucking true. You can't abandon someone when you don't know where the hell they are and he had no idea where Carmody went, no idea at all.

*Oh, you know, man. You know. He went up in the trees like that gook officer. You know he did. And what kind of thing do you think could take Gunny that quick, that silently?*

But the answer to that question he did not want to know.

If he made it back, he was going to have to cook up some bullshit story or they'd lock him up in a psych ward.

He finished his cigarette and started taking bearings. When he got back into the heavier jungle, he'd get his compass out. He knew where the LZ was. He would wait there until morning, then pop green smoke when he heard the chopper coming. But first, he had to get there.

He started moving.

He was in some kind of field inundated in deep mud. He would push for the treeline due east. He slogged on for another fifteen minutes until the vegetation around him grew thicker, then he paused.

He heard a sound in a clump of brush off to his left and opened up on it. No economy or precision here, just jerking that trigger and firing on full-auto like he'd been doing for hours now. Starting at the slightest sound. Like some cherry two weeks in-country. He kept moving, falling into the muck and dragging himself up. The jungle was alive with the sounds of big predators. His teeth were chattering and he was cold and soaked to the skin. The mud was up above his knees now and it was chill and slimy, down in his boots and up his pants, splattered in his face.

He kept thinking: *That valley, that goddamned valley like some kind of graveyard and that thing, that goddamned thing hunting in the trees—*

And then through the pouring sheets of rain he could see eight or ten dark figures fanning out, encircling him. NVA or VC? Maybe an ARVN patrol or Americans or ROKs or Australians. Maybe just smugglers or bandits out to rob and murder.

But the figures closed and Spiers could see their helmets.

NVA. No doubt.

Stands of wiry bushes grew up from the flooded undergrowth and Spiers went down behind one, even though he was certain they'd spotted him. They kept coming closer and they moved...*strangely,* without any unit discipline. Just men with guns out walking, fanning out.

When they were thirty feet away, he started shooting.

He used economical three-round bursts and cut down two of them before the others started shooting back. And then it was the rain and the hammering of AKs and muzzle flashes and men crying out and Spiers made a break for it, shooting from the hip as water splashed and slugs ripped apart the foliage and one stray round grazed his thigh. He was marooned in a sea of sluicing mud that came up to his hips and maybe it was quicksand, because he was trapped. His rifle clicked on an empty chamber and something like a burning white-hot blade slit across his temple and he fell face-forward into the muck, his head full of pain. Thrashing and fighting, he pulled his face out of the mud, waiting for a tossed stick grenade to end him.

But it didn't happen.

Three NVA slipped into the mire with him. He cracked one with the butt of his rifle and sent him sprawling. Then other rifle butts glanced off his own skull and down he went.

He felt himself sinking helplessly in the mud.

A voice in his head said: *You're dead, Spiers, you're fucking meat now. This means a malarial POW jungle camp where you can waste away. You ain't no pilot, you ain't worth anything to Hanoi, you're no bargaining chip. They won't send you north, they'll just let you die…*

The NVA dragged him out of there by the feet into the wet grass, constantly pounding and beating him until he trembled on the edge of consciousness. He looked up once and someone kicked him in the nuts and another stomped his head with a boot heel. They kept working him until he teetered helplessly in some blank, hopeless zone just this side of reality. They bound his hands behind his back and forced his face down into the muck again. His mouth was full of that foul gray mud. It was in his eyes, up his nose.

He kept trying to speak, swallowing clots of that cool slime.

His captors asked him no questions. They dragged him by the feet through the dripping undergrowth face-down, leaves and loose clods of gorse mashed into his nostrils. Sticks and jutting roots cut gashes in his cheeks, split open his lips.

And onward they went, Spiers finally passing out.

# 10

He languished in a bamboo tiger cage for ten days.

At first, he was pretty delirious and wasn't even sure where he was. He had a waking/sleeping/dreaming nightmare complete with the shakes and cold sweats that he was still in that goddamn valley, that he couldn't find his way out and that *thing* was after him as he crawled on his hands and knees through bamboo thickets. He remembered waking a few times, thinking he had heard screams. He was certain the leering full moon above was the eye of the creature that had taken Carmody.

It went on and on.

Other times, he was certain that he was back home in Missouri and the war had never happened. It was all so real. He was hanging out with his friends and dating girls at the drive-in and sitting around with his mom and dad at night watching silly shit like *Get Smart* and *The Red Skelton Hour.* He could almost feel the summer sun as he cruised the strip with one arm hanging out the window of his candy apple red '65 Skylark. The whole scenario was as perfect as the nightmare of the valley had been horrible.

But it had to end.

All good things must.

When he opened his eyes for real, it was daylight and his back was aching. He was thirsty and hungry and generally sore, but he wasn't too bad off for that. The air was heavy and humid, water dripping from the bamboo crossbars above. A brown bug about the size of a cigar butt was crawling up his leg and he flicked it free. He was still wearing his boots and jungle utilities. Usually, from what he had heard, the Viets stripped them right away and gave you foul-smelling black pajamas to wear.

The camp was set in a little clearing of shorn grasses, puddles of brown mud everywhere. There were no huts for the guards or quarters for the commander that he could see which meant it was a transitional camp, a temporary holding area. The sort of place where rounded-up POWs were sent until it was safe enough for the

NVA to herd them farther north, maybe up past the DMZ where the chances of rescue by American commandos was less likely. Within a few days or a week at the outside, he figured, he and the other prisoners would be marched to another camp deep in the jungle, perhaps over the border into Cambodia where American units could not follow.

There was no tree cover above. Any chopper flying over would scope the compound out and report it to command. That wasn't how the VC/NVA usually did it. They liked to tuck their temporary camps away under triple-canopy jungle so they could not be observed by low-flying aircraft. This location made no sense.

*Sense?* he asked himself. *Can you really, honestly be looking for sense in things after that fucking valley?*

But that made him think of Gunny Carmody and it filled his throat with a rising bubble of emotion. He swallowed it back down. God knew he missed that SOB, but now was hardly the time for mourning or a good crying jag. He had to keep it together. His job now, as a POW, was escape. He had to start thinking hard in that direction and preferably before they moved him again and the navigating got that much more difficult.

He peered through the bamboo bars of his prison, taking it all in.

What he could see of it told him what he already knew: that this was purely a temporary, half-assed operation. There could have been accommodations for the guards off in the jungle, but he had the strangest feeling that what he was seeing was all that there was. He counted at least a dozen other cages, but none of them were close enough so that the prisoners could communicate or even see each other.

There was a perimeter of punji stakes smeared with shit surrounding the makeshift compound. Their tips were facing inward in order to impale any escaping prisoner. The feces, once introduced to the body, would create a raging infection. The forest just beyond was set with tall trees and what looked like an impenetrable wall of encroaching jungle: snaking vines and immense ferns, crowded bamboo thickets and huge banyans, wild banana trees and thorny vegetation.

Spiers knew if he could slip away, his best bet would be to crawl through the jungle rather than try and escape through the clearing. Once he was in the brush, it would be very hard for them to find him. He saw five or six NVA guards in dirty, ragged khaki uniforms and well-worn pith helmets. They carried AK-47s, but they looked despondent to a man, weary and beaten. One of them saw him looking and jogged away into the jungle.

*Shit, here it comes.*

What came was a stubby little Viet whose face scowled even when he didn't. Spiers figured he was the commander of the garrison, but it was possible he was some kind of political commissar or intelligence type. He wore the same uniform as the others but without identifiable insignia of any sort. He carried a riding crop like a Japanese commandant and lacked the ability to speak English in normal tones. He stormed up to Spiers' cage and smacked his crop against the bars. "YOU!" he shouted. "YOU ARE AN AMERICAN WAR CRIMINAL! YOU ARE A YANKEE RAPIST DESPOILING THE HOMELAND! YOU ARE A PRISONER OF THE VIETNAM PEOPLE'S ARMY! YOU WILL NOT SPEAK UNLESS SPOKEN TO! YOU WILL FOLLOW ALL ORDERS TO THE LETTER OR THE PUNISHMENT WILL BE SEVERE!"

Spiers just sat there while he raged on and on about all the things he couldn't do—which were many—and all the things he could do—which were few. All the while, he was thinking that if it wasn't for the cage and the guards, he would have kicked that little prick from one end of the compound to the other. If such a chance were ever given him, which was highly unlikely, he might just do it for laughs.

The little shit got himself worked into such a foaming fury, he left without introducing himself which was a real fucking pity as far as Spiers was concerned. As he stormed back across the compound, he shouted in Vietnamese at his guards. When he was gone, he could tell by the looks on their faces that he wasn't real popular with the enlisted guys.

About an hour later, a guard came over with a large wooden bowl of something that smelled most foul. Spiers recognized it as *nuoc-mam,* which was sort of a rice soup with vegetables and tiny little fish like minnows. The Viets put it in jars and buried it until it was well-fermented. He had seen them digging it up around the firebase. More than one of them had been blown away at the firebase when a perimeter guard thought they were burying a mine.

The door was unlocked and the bowl was handed to him. "Eat," the guard said. "This good."

Well, that was a matter of opinion. He supposed like the Scandinavians and their lutefisk it was a matter of taste. But he ate it. It stank to high heaven, but he knew if he poured it out or refused it, the guard would take offense and he probably wouldn't see so much as a handful of rice for many days to come. He swallowed it down, wincing at the fishy taste it left in his mouth and the slime that coated his throat. It took some concentration on his part to *keep* it down.

When he was done, there was nothing to do but watch what went on in camp, which was absolutely nothing, and kill insects that tried to invade his happy home. What he tried most not to think about was his future which was bleak.

And what happened in the valley.

Especially not that.

# ⚶

When he first got in-country, Spiers saw the people as being Vietnamese. Simple, honest farmers who were just trying to wrestle a living from the soil. After his first firefight, they were all fucking gooks and he wanted to kill them.

His original assessment was that they were different in many ways from Americans, but they all seemed to want peace and prosperity, abundant crops to feed their families and good lives for their children. He understood that and tried to be compassionate to them. The Vietnamese were just people, that's all. No better or no worse than anyone else. This was the sort of thing that was pounded in his head before he got over there and he tried to keep on thinking it even though, day by day, he believed it even less.

The thing that changed it for him was not so much the firefight on Hill 77—like Blueberry Hill, he had his thrill and lost his cherry there—but the aftermath of it. A Marine Recon platoon got pinned down up there and fought hard through the night, trading blows with a hard-bitten company of NVA regulars. The Recon platoon had not gone up there to get in a pissing contest with a numerically superior enemy force but merely to set up an Observation Post to monitor enemy activity in the area. The NVA did not like an OP in their sector and decided they were going to do something about it.

The Recon platoon were tenacious as hell and they would not give in or lie down and die. They were stubborn but so were the NVA. The NVA wanted that hill. God knows why, one hill looking pretty much like another. Maybe because it was the only hill that was still forested. The others were all stripped and dead and horribly gutted. Some of that was from artillery strikes and bombing runs from Phantom jets, but most of it was from an Air Force unit called the "Ranch Hands"—*Only we can prevent forests*—that saturated the area with defoliants.

The battle raged on through the night and the Marines called in airstrikes against the entrenched enemy that were absolutely devastating, but by dawn the NVA managed to overrun their position and all eighteen Marines were either killed outright or wounded badly. Spiers had been with the reaction force that was choppered in a few klicks west of the hill. Two Marine companies charged in and wiped out nearly all the remaining NVA. Their dead were everywhere, mangled corpses and parts of them spread out over the dead defoliated countryside, the remains of the once lush forests that blanketed the area reduced to gray, crumbling debris. The NVA usually like to sanitize a battlefield by removing their dead and their equipment to reinforce the myth of their own indestructibility (which was complete bullshit because any American unit that caught them out in the open knew, in fact, how very destructible they were). But there had been no time with the reaction force bearing down on them.

Spiers walked amongst their corpses, many of which had been lying around for more than twelve hours and were swollen and juicy like ripe fruit in the tropical heat. When they got to Hill 77, all the Marines were dead. Though several had been KIA, most had just been wounded. They would probably have survived except the NVA had bayoneted them all.

One of the jarheads who saw that went absolutely wild. He started raging and shouting, foaming at the mouth and screaming at the top of his lungs. "FUCKING *ANIMALS!* FUCKING MURDERING GUTLESS COWARDLY MOTHERFUCKING ANIMALS! FUCKING GOOKS! FUCKING SLOPE ZIPPERHEAD DINK SLANT-EYED COCKSUCKERS! YOU DON'T DO THAT TO INJURED MEN! YOU DON'T...FUCKING...DO...THAT!"

The guy had to be sedated and taken away before he went charging off to kill some Viets. Friend or enemy, he would have cut them up.

But Spiers knew where he was coming from.

He couldn't wrap his brain around that. *Bayoneting the wounded.* That was sick, it was fucked up, it was cowardly... which meant the Viets had to be all sick, fucked up and cowardly. So from that moment on, he decided they were all diseased animals that needed to be put down.

It made things so much easier.

# R

There was nothing to do but wait.

It was a strange place even by the standards of a temporary POW camp. He'd known other grunts that had been held by the North Viets or Southern VC irregulars and their experiences were quite different from his own. They seemed to talk of endless beatings, starvation, torture…but Spiers got none of that, or almost none. They were feeding him and generally ignoring him, which was more than a little unsettling. Other than the dressing down he'd gotten from the commandant—if that's what that loud-mouthed little prick was—he'd had very little interaction with any of them.

It made him suspicious.

It made him wonder if something bad was in the wind, if maybe they were keeping him fresh and unmolested so they could turn him over to professional interrogators that would tear him apart.

Maybe. Possibly. But he didn't believe it.

There were fifteen other cages.

They were spread out in a little clearing, just within the perimeter of the jungle, so he couldn't see the other prisoners. But he could hear them and especially at night—moaning and whimpering and crying out. Other than that, they were gray forms crowded in those little cages where there was not enough room to lay down or stand-up. Spiers learned and learned very quickly to sleep crouched over.

The compound was weirdly silent day and night, save for the little guy yelling from time to time.

His third day there, a guard—a dour-faced creature with drab, empty eyes and all the vitality of an automaton—brought his food (a healthy portion of rice, boiled vegetables, and some sort of spicy meat which was surprisingly quite good). Spiers, using what little Vietnamese he knew, asked him where it was he was being held and what the commandant's plans were. Obvious, routine questions from the incarcerated.

But they enraged the guard.

He pulled out a stick and started working over Spiers with it until his head had more lumps in it than grandma's gravy and his left eye was swollen shut. Spiers let him have his fun. If it hadn't been for the two guys with the AKs standing behind him, he would've shoved that stick so far up the shrimp's ass it would've tickled the back of his throat.

Lesson learned…or maybe not.

His fourth day there, he tried to call out to another prisoner and one of the guards heard him. Three of them came out of nowhere and dragged Spiers out into the broiling sunshine and gave him a going over with bamboo poles that whistled as they cut the air. After five minutes of that, his legs covered in welts, his face a livid bruise, his stomach twisted into knots, they tossed him back into the cage.

But the really crazy, really weird thing was that after the beating, some gook came and bandaged his wounds, rubbed salve on him, and made him drink some tea that was laced with alcohol.

In broken English, he said, "Quiet. Must always be quiet."

Once again, it seemed like the only thing that enraged them was if he opened his mouth. At first, he thought it was because they were afraid that American or ARVN forces might hear him, but as the days passed he was not so sure of that. They were afraid of something and he did not honestly think it was friendly forces.

Something was going on.

Something strange.

*You're thinking about that fucking valley. You're thinking there's a connection…but what possible connection can there be?*

He couldn't think of one, but it didn't mean it wasn't there.

After the valley, the war had an entirely different complexion. He didn't think he'd ever be able to look at it quite the same way again.

Another thing he found increasingly disturbing was that the guards didn't even speak amongst themselves. They were a silent bunch and seemed to communicate solely through gestures and nods of their heads. They were not just cowed but frightened.

Nothing made any sense.

Not from the plentiful food they gave him to the nearly mild treatment to the buckets of water they fetched from some well in the jungle, always purifying it with tablets before they let him drink it. Again, unheard of. Most POWs (and many VC) had amebic dysentery and five or six varieties of the screaming shits that hadn't even been classified as yet. But here he was with good food, good water, even medicine. One of the guards even gave him cigarettes if he kept his mouth shut. American cigarettes.

*"You smoke now,"* he'd say. *"You smoke and be quiet. No noise. No noise at all. Ssshhh."*

Go figure.

The accommodations left something to be desired, but other than that it was hardly hell on earth. Spiers thought maybe they were keeping him healthy until a main force arrived and he was smuggled out of South Vietnam…but, again, he just didn't believe that.

The guards were a lean, emaciated lot with blotchy skin and hollowed cheeks. They drank water from puddles and ate rancid-looking rice with foul-smelling fish sauce. He ate much better than they did.

He kept quiet and made sure he finished all his meals—the guards got pissy and violent if he didn't—and time passed. Slowly, very slowly, but it did pass.

The nights were cool and damp, the days blistering hot. He would lay there listening to commotion out in the jungle—birds and monkeys and insects, a solid, unwavering wall of noise—as his mind kept turning it all over and over. Here he was, stuck in a cage, but not being beaten if he kept his mouth shut. He was fed, looked after, rewarded with cigarettes. It didn't make any sense, but then nothing much did by that point. It really wasn't that long since Carmody and he were out hunting dinks. Seemed even less since they'd gone down into that valley and, and—

That really bothered him.

Had he really experienced any of that? The VC getting snatched by something in the trees? Carmody vanishing? That awful, resounding roar when he'd slipped out of the valley?

He kept telling himself that he must have picked something up, some tropical fever perhaps, and had hallucinated the entire thing. But he couldn't make himself believe that, of course. It was all still too vivid in his mind and he knew there was something in that valley, something terrible and unnatural. If he escaped tomorrow and made it back to an American unit and home, he knew that forty years from now he'd still believe it.

The fifth night, he saw something else unusual.

Just after dark, a group of guards came with long poles and slid them through one of the cages, carrying it off into the jungle. Within twenty minutes, a sound split the air—the same droning siren-like sound he had heard in the valley. It kept rising in the night, higher and higher, until it took on the quality of a frenzied wailing like a fire whistle. Then it faded away completely.

A few hours later, the guards brought the cage back empty. The next night, they carried off three cages, the occupants screaming and throwing themselves against the bars. Then again, came the sound of the siren cycling out of the jungle. Of those three cages, two came back empty. The third held a man just as shrunken and drained as those mummies with the stakes up their asses. He laid there moaning and whining pitifully, but the fight was gone out of him. As they carried his cage by, Spiers noticed that he was slimed with some snotty, viscous substance like mucus or jelly. Tangles of the stuff were twined between the bars of the cage. The next night they took him out again and the siren shrilled.

He did not come back.

By the seventh night, this was becoming a regular occurrence. Spiers didn't care for it at all, because he knew his turn was coming sooner or later. But he kept his mouth shut and bided his time, hoping that if he was a good little prisoner the guards might get a little freer with him and when that happened, he was either getting out or he was going to die trying. Regardless, there was no damn way they were taking him out into the jungle to whatever unknown, unpleasant fate awaited him.

It was something to cling to.

## 13

His ninth night in captivity, a storm blew up. Lightning flashed and thunder boomed and rain came down in blinding sheets. The clearing became a river that lapped at the cages. Water ran through the bars overhead in gushing streams. Spiers was sitting there, waiting for them to take out the cages, but they never did. The guards hid under trees and tried to wait it out, but the storm raged on and on.

The air suddenly went cooler by degrees, seemed sluggish and heavy. The rain stirred up everything, inundating the jungle in a fresh, green smell. But there was suddenly another odor drifting into camp—a viscid, crawling stench of spoiled meat.

Something about it made him go tense.

It was very strong, almost gagging, like the hot breath of an animal that had been chewing on carrion. But it was worse than that because just underneath it there was another odor, a dark sweetness that made his belly go weak and made his skin feel tight on his bones. The rain kept pouring down, running into his cage, and if it hadn't been for that he would have been sweating because he was scared, unbelievably scared.

The stink was the same thing he'd smelled in the valley.

He was sure of it.

The guards started running around, looking confused, looking frightened. The little Viet came out and shouted things at them. The rain was falling too loudly so Spiers couldn't quite make out what it was. His Vietnamese was barely functional so he probably wouldn't have understood it anyway, but he could easily sense the panic and mounting terror in the man's voice.

The guards ran off into the jungle and the little Viet followed them. Then there was just the rain and the cages and that building, repulsive stench that seemed to have a life of its own, a breathing, sentient other.

The siren shrilled again, sounding like the menacing cry of some prehistoric raptor. This time it wasn't merely one long, sustained cry, but a series of them. It sounded angry.

Spiers sat there, terrified and shaking, nearly feverish with mounting dread. He could barely draw a breath. He was wet and shivering, his mouth dry as autumn leaves.

He was thinking: *These cages, we're trapped in these fucking cages and it's coming, Christ in Heaven, it's coming…*

And it was.

A huge and tenebrous motion. A slithering, a whispering, an eldritch rustling of something that should not be but was. His hands gripped the splintered bamboo bars and his eyes were shut because he didn't want to look, didn't want to see whatever was coming because if he saw it he would lose his mind.

The rain still poured down, but it had taken on a muted sound as thunder rumbled like an empty belly and lightning flashed, strobing the wet landscape with ephemeral glimpses of an electric, blinding daylight.

The flesh along the back of his neck was creeping. His scalp had gone tight. He could hear the other poor bastards in their cages moaning and yelling and rattling their bars, because they *felt* it coming, too. The air was vibrant now with an inexorable lunacy.

Closer.

Moving through the sodden, primordial jungle with a huge, clicking sound, a living and determined sound. A sliding, a slithering, a rending. Branches were breaking and underbrush was crackling. The ground seemed to vibrate with hidden life. Closer it came and closer still, the air redolent with a warm, greasy smell like noisome pork simmering in the sun.

The lightning was flashing and Spiers felt the thing's nearness, the pressure of its form that turned the air thin and suffocating, sucking the oxygen from it, exciting the molecules maybe, turning the world into some putrid envelope of malignance. He forced his eyes open, deciding he would see, had to see.

The world exploded with glaring illumination from the lightning.

And he saw…thought he saw…something immense push itself through the slate-gray curtain of rain and dripping jungle. Whatever it was, it was damn fast, moving with a furtive, spidery motion. And then the darkness covered it again and he couldn't be sure if it had only been a tangle of shadows or wind-blown jungle his mind had sculpted into something else entirely.

But he could still smell it.

He could *feel* it in his head.

And he was aware that it was very close now, maybe close enough to touch. The lightning flashed again in rapid succession like fireworks and he was staring fearfully across camp at a cage maybe a hundred feet away and…and something oily and pale and undulating crept out of the forest, moving towards it. He didn't know what it was, but it was big, unnatural, and its eyes shined like glass. Then someone screamed and there was a great, horrible hissing sound that rose to a feverish pitch…then only the wind and the rain and an odd sense of *vacancy*.

Maybe ten seconds later, the lightning exploded again and Spiers saw that the cage was gone. But in the next flash, he saw it wasn't gone exactly, just shattered into kindling and dumped at the threshold of the jungle.

Whatever had slipped into camp, had slipped back out again, its belly full.

After that, Spiers did not close his eyes at night.

He waited for the guards to take his cage away and he waited for the nights when the weather was bad and the thing from the jungle came in person. His life before the camp grew gray and indistinct and he wondered sometimes if he'd only dreamed it, that maybe he'd always been in this cage waiting for an unspeakable death. The guards wandered about like living skeletons, never speaking, feeding him in silence, offering him cigarettes and watching him with dead eyes that did not seem to see.

And then, it happened.

One night just after sunset—his tenth night to be exact and a night he was certain was *his* night to be introduced to what lived in the dark recesses of the forest—he suddenly became aware of activity in the jungle. Maybe those living dead guards didn't pick up on it, but Spiers did. You spent enough time tracking men, you knew when they were out stalking. Somebody was sneaking around the perimeter of the camp.

One of the guards slipped into the bushes to take a piss and Spiers saw a dark form slip up behind him, snap his head back and slip a knife into his throat. Then more forms slipped out of the jungle and there was the hollow popping of silenced weapons. Within three minutes, the guards were all dead. Those that hadn't been shot, were knifed or garroted.

One of the forms came up to Spiers' cage and Spiers saw the green-painted face, the boonie hat, and then a machete cut open the bars and a voice said, "It's time to get the fuck outta Dodge, troop."

At the Bien Hoa Tactical Airbase, some fifteen minutes north of Saigon by helicopter, Spiers spent the next month in the hospital. Physically, he wasn't in bad condition other than the swelling from bug bites and a mild tropical fever that the medics brought under control with antibiotics within twenty-four hours. He figured they could've sprung him the third day, but they didn't and he knew why.

They thought he was crazy.

He'd been rescued, he learned, by Force Recon Marines. Along with the SEALs and Green Beret SOG units, they were considered to be the very best of that war's shadow warriors. Intelligence had received word of the POW camp and a seven-man Force Recon Stingray Team had been sent in. They took down twelve guards in less time than it takes to tell. They dragged Spiers, another American, and six other Viets through the jungle where they were extracted by a pair of slicks and flown to the air base.

Once there, Spiers told them his story.

He knew it was a wild tale, but ten days in a POW camp had pretty much softened his perceptions of what people would believe and what they wouldn't. Day after day, military psychiatrists made him tell his story. And, eventually, frustrated and angered by that condescending, pitying look in their eyes, he started saying he couldn't remember what had happened. They didn't believe him, but he refused to speak anymore of it.

He wanted only two things by then: out of the hospital and out of the Marine Corps. One of the doctors told him he could probably swing a psychological discharge pretty easily. In other words, Spiers was so fucking crazy the Marines would be glad to be rid of his nutty ass.

And that's how it was for him: day in, day out, psychiatrists and guys in suits and guys in fatigues with no insignia—CIA spooks, he was thinking—coming to see him and asking him questions about what he'd seen, what happened to NCO Master Gunnery Sergeant Carmody, about the POW camp, and if they'd encountered any build-ups of VC or NVA. Same bullshit day after day. Carmody was listed, he learned, as KIA-BNR—Killed In Action-Body Not Recovered.

After he was there a week, ready to jump out of his skin, a Marine major walked into the ward and took him off into an office where they could talk.

"You remember me, Corporal?"

Spiers told him he did. "You led the team that sprung me. I never had time to thank you guys, sir. I never—"

"I don't want thanks. It's my job." His name was Wick and he had lifer written all over him. He had the requisite thick neck and pickle-jar head topped by sharp, bristly gray hair. His eyes glistened like wet steel. "Don't take that the wrong way. But I didn't do it as a personal favor."

"Well, you got my thanks anyway."

Wick grunted. "Are you so sure you *want* to thank me?"

"I don't understand, sir."

Wick smiled thinly. "Sure you do. You understand me just fine. We plucked you out of the camp and locked you in here. You can't tell me you like the way they treat you in this place. Keeping you in the psych ward with all the other head-cases. It's okay, Corporal, relax, you can talk to me."

Spiers wasn't so sure about that, but he figured he owed this guy something. "No, I don't like it, sir. I saw what I saw and nobody believes me. At first, I couldn't wait to get back to my company…"

"But now?"

Spiers lit a cigarette, stared out the window. "Now, I just want out. Out of this fucking country, out of the Corps. I don't like people saying I'm a liar."

Wick thought about that for a few moments. "You sticking to that business about the monster?"

"Sure. I'm nuts, sir. I don't know any better."

"I think you do." Wick was drumming his fingers on the desk. He studied his hands, then looked up at Spiers, a haunted look falling over his eyes. "About a year ago, give or take, I took a 14-man recon platoon up North, just this side of Quang Tri. An NVA division was dug in deep up there and the Army Air Cav got a bloody nose trying to drag their asses out…so, the B-52s went in and bombed the living hell out of them. Preliminary word was that the NVA suffered something like seventy-percent causalities and withdrew. We parachuted in there to perform a bomb damage assessment. Pretty standard stuff, right?"

Spiers just shrugged, dragging slowly off his cigarette.

Wick told him it was hard to put into words what they'd seen up there. The landscape looked like the dark side of the moon—bomb craters as far as the eye could see. The jungle had been blasted flat and those craters were twenty-feet across and five, six feet deep, sometimes more. It was the rainy season and they were filled with water and leeches and snakes, Wick said. The moon kept slipping out from behind clouds and lighting up the countryside and there were bodies (and parts of them) everywhere—half-buried in the mud, floating in the water, blown up into the leafless trees. Rats had come out and were feeding on them.

"I had three guys in my squad, Spiers, and we were swimming our way through a crater, pushing aside bodies that were bloated up like barrels and just putrid smelling. You were afraid to bump them because they might burst and let all that gas out…and the smell…Jesus," Wick remembered, looking positively ill. "We made it across and we're creeping up the rim of the crater like a couple of kids coming out of a wading pool when we hear something. Movement. We slip back into the muck and wait. The moon comes out and shows us something we didn't want or need to see—about thirty feet away, in another crater filled with floating bodies, this shape comes up out of the water. Right away, see, we knew it wasn't a gook. Shit, it wasn't even *human*. Just this little hunched-up thing with long arms and a mouthful of sharp teeth. It turned and looked at us, the moon shining in its face and I could see it had only one eye, one big ugly eye set in a face would've made Dr. Frankenstein puke. It saw us and we saw it, then it grabbed one of the NVA corpses and slid back under the water with it. It never came back up."

Spiers was just looking at him, his cigarette paused before his lips. "You serious?"

Wick nodded. "All I'm saying is weird shit happens in this war, happens in all wars. Did I ever tell anybody about it? Hell, no.

Don't plan to either. Myself and three others saw that thing plain enough. But we've kept it to ourselves."

Spiers took his drag now. "In other words, if I had half a brain, sir, I would have kept *my* story to myself, too?"

"Save you some grief," Wick said. "That's all I'm saying, corporal."

Wick explained to him if he ever repeated that story—the bomb-crater story—to anyone, he'd deny it and then he'd kick his ass. Enough said.

"So, tell me," he began. "What in the name of Christ were you and your sergeant doing in Cambodia? Last I heard, that wasn't our Area of Operations."

"Ain't nobody's AO," Spiers said. "Just that thing's."

He told Wick about it best he could. He made it sound like it was a mutual decision and not just Carmody's obsession to bag that officer. "And now he's dead and I want out. I've had my fill."

Wick just nodded. "You want out, eh? Well, way I see it, you've got a choice. Because only two things can happen here. You can get your discharge, but you're going to be sent stateside to Bethesda for psychiatric evaluation. Something like that could go on for months and months…"

"And what's the second thing?"

"You can accompany my team on a little operation into Cambodia. Into this valley you lost NCO Carmody in."

Spiers just stared at him, waiting for the punchline that never came. Of course it never came—because *he* was the punchline. "No goddamn way! No fucking way I'm going back out there, sir. You don't understand, you haven't been there, you don't know—"

"Good," Wick said. "We leave tomorrow night. You make it back and you're processed out."

It took Spiers awhile before he opened his mouth and when he did, he said, "Since when does Force Recon go monster-hunting, sir?"

"Monsters? What monsters?" He had fallen right back into military cadence again. "What we've got out there is a fortified NVA unit, possibly elements of a VC sapper battalion. Our mission is to locate them, route them out. Find 'em, fix 'em, and fuck 'em. Welcome aboard, son."

ƀ

If nothing else, it got him out of the hospital.

He found the enlisted man's club and started throwing back shots of Jim Beam until his head was thrumming with an easy, pleasant buzz. He sat there on a barstool, staring at the rows of liquor bottles lined up like soldiers and remembering real things in the real world—girls he'd known, his hometown, the ballpark, football on a blustery late September afternoon. He just stared into dead space with chipped-stone eyes that might've been plucked from a gargoyle perched precariously in some high, windy spot. And, like that gargoyle, he was only holding on by his toes.

"You planning on getting shit-faced?" a voice asked.

Spiers whipped his head around, spilling his drink. A Marine NCO was standing there and by the colorful patch on his jungle fatigues—skull and crossbones—there was no doubt he was with the Force Recon detachment. He was a small, muscular man with heavy forearms and a face that was pitted with shrapnel scars and a throat scarfed with old burn tissue.

"That's what I was planning on doing, sir," Spiers said.

"I'm Master Gunnery Sergeant Rice," the man said. "I'm the senior NCO with Team Red Shadow, First Force Reconnaissance Company. And you must be Lance Corporal Spiers. Eight months in-country, Scout-Sniper. Outstanding. You belong to me now. Let's go."

Within ten minutes—ten minutes in which Rice told him what a shit-useless disgrace to the Corps he indeed was—they were out on the tarmac, climbing aboard a Marine Huey. Twenty minutes later they were touching down at Firebase Smith on the Mekong River. The other Marines there, just your average grunts, gave Rice a wide berth and looked at Spiers like they pitied him. On the far side of the compound, encircled by concertina wire and sandbags, were a series of bunkers cut into the earth. The home of Team Red Shadow. Behind the bunkers, strung from the wire like ghoulish marionettes were eight or ten Viet Cong corpses, all blackened to leather.

"Why doesn't somebody cut them down for chrissake?" Spiers said.

Rice shrugged. "We're hoping the VC will some night. In fact, we *dare* them to."

Jesus.

Spiers didn't like the place, didn't like the stink of death or those crazy-looking Recons with their bald-heads and ritual tattooing. One guy sported a Mohawk and another had his face and shaven head tattooed with black tiger stripes. Rice brought him down into the command bunker and had him sit on some stacked ammo crates right next to a dirty fish aquarium half-filled with things like curled, brown November leaves. Spiers realized they were human ears.

Trophy hunters. He'd heard that about the spec ops units.

A guy with a long black scalp lock which was surely not regulation came up to him right away. He wore no shirt and was bronzed by the sun. Spiers thought he might have been an Indian. He jabbed a finger in Spiers' chest. "You know what my name is?"

Spiers shook his head. "No."

The guy just sneered at him. "Good, let's keep it that way." And walked away.

And that was just one of them. They were a real collection of cold-blooded psychos, looking more like mercenaries than Marines. He recognized a few from when they liberated the POW camp. They stood around staring at him like hyenas considering a joint of meat until Major Wick came in and told them to get the fuck out. He introduced Spiers to another sergeant, this one named Nordstrom, but known on the Team as "Swede." Swede took him to another bunker and cracked a few cans of Tiger beer for them.

"Don't let that bunch bother you," he told Spiers. "You're the Fucking New Guy. They're always hard on the FNGs. Real clannish these guys. Been here too long. Command keeps 'em over here on account there's nothing else these guys can do but kill people. They're crazy. Guys like these…what the fuck they gonna do back in the world? Killers, they don't know shit about real life. Not like me and you, normal guys." Swede had eyes like black, reflective glass. He wore the typical Marine crew cut, but sported a Fu Manchu mustache that reached well below his jaw line. Just your average Joe. He had a K-Bar knife and was meticulously trimming the hair off the back of his hand. "You know what the greatest fear of those animals is?"

Spiers shook his head. He couldn't imagine men like that being afraid of anything.

Swede pulled off his beer. "They're afraid that the war will end."

Spiers didn't doubt that at all. He just couldn't see these guys going back home and working in a factory or a car wash. Not without a body count.

"Wick tell you what we're going to do?"

Spiers said, "Sure. I got the official line. We're hunting a NVA/VC unit."

"That's what he said?" Swede thought that was funny. "You were in that valley, so you know what we're after. I've never been there, but I was in a village about three klicks from there."

Swede told him all about it like they'd been friends for years.

It was a place called Con Lo. A shit-nothing little ville, Swede told him. Right away, they knew something was funny. The place looked dead, looked haunted with the mist spilling down over it from the hills. It had all the ambience of an open grave. They waited and watched for a few hours and saw no activity. But soon as they moved down the ridge, about two dozen Viets came up out of the grass. Swede said they couldn't tell if they were just tribal mercs or VC hardcore or maybe a little of both or goddamn neither. They carried AKs and old French carbines and even a few Swedish Ks. They had no military bearing, no discipline. They charged the Force Recons and within ten minutes, they were all dead, cut to shit. A thoroughly psychotic, fanatical lot.

"Motherfuckers, Spiers, lunatic motherfuckers," Swede told him. "We put 'em down and right away any of 'em with any life left in them came charging right up at us. You had guys with arms blown off, holes in their chests, guts hanging out coming at us with their bare hands. Slope with his face blown back to bone jumped on me and I had to stab him about thirty goddamn times before he went still…"

After that, Swede said, they slipped down into the village. It was empty. They didn't find any of the usual shit—no maps or documents or radios or weapons caches. Nothing at all unless you wanted to count a trench filled with maybe thirty, forty bodies— Viets, Cambodes, Americans. And all of them shrunken and leathery. A preliminary examination showed one thing—not a one had any blood in them. Not a drop. And they all had strange, circular marks on them.

"Like those pictures you see of whales with sucker scars from squids," Swede explained to him, his voice gone low and hollow. "We found something like an altar out back of the hootches. Chains there like maybe they chained up people, sacrificed 'em or some shit."

Spiers just sat there, a headache developing behind his eyes. He told Swede about the POW camp he'd been in. What it was like there. "I knew, sooner or later, my cage was going into the jungle and I wouldn't be coming back."

Swede just nodded. "And you know why they treated you so good, right? You know why you got fed so much?"

"Sure," Spiers said in a whisper, his skin feeling very tight. "They were fattening me up…for that thing."

## 6

A CH-46 dropped them in a clearing about two klicks from the valley at 0500 hours.

It came down quick and then the team was running down the ramp into the chest-high elephant grass. The wash from the spinning rotors was so intense it nearly sucked Spiers off his feet. And then they were alone in the darkness and the Chinook was up and gone and the night closed in around them.

Quiet. Very quiet.

They moved off into the jungle, methodically scanning the trees ahead with Starlight scopes and carefully placing their feet down before stepping. There were ten of them in Team Red Shadow including Major Wick. U.S. forces were openly forbidden from entering Cambodia, so the team carried "sterile" weapons: Chicom Type-56 variants of the AK-47 assault rifle, French MAT-49 submachine guns, modified Tokarev auto pistols, and two Russian RPD 7.62 mm light machine guns with the barrels sawed-off short. There were also a pair of semi-auto Soviet Dragunov sniper rifles, one of which was given to Spiers, the other to Swede. Each man packed 300 rounds of ammo, fragmentation and white phosphorus grenades, machetes, fighting knives, and an assortment of personalized equipment ranging from short-barreled shotguns to garrotes.

They were an odd assortment, some wearing nylon jungle boots and others running shoes, some in jungle fatigues and others in VC-type black jammies, some with soft boonie hats and others in bandannas. Wick and the Indian with the ponytail held two LAW rocket launchers. And they all carried thirty-feet of rope and rappelling harnesses.

Spiers didn't even ask about the rocket launchers; maybe he didn't want to know.

The only things he was particularly interested in were the small crystal radios that both Wick and Rice carried. They were capable of sending, not receiving. A Forward Air Controller would be listening for the signal to pick them up. When the FAC received it, he'd scramble choppers to the main and secondary extraction LZs—and when the Force Recons popped the right color smoke, down they'd come.

Before they hopped aboard the chopper, Wick took Spiers aside and said, "Listen up. Shit hits the fan, you might find yourself alone or with a bunch of wounded men. Our call sign is Tango Ten-Five. You got that? Tango Ten-Five. You need extraction, you call for Green Garden and pop orange smoke. You need an airstrike, you call for Papa Nickel. Give 'em the coordinates and they'll rain Armageddon down. That's it. That's all you got to know if things get bad."

Spiers memorized it all: *Tango Ten-Five. Green Garden. Orange smoke. Papa Nickel.* Easy.

The guy with the scalp lock took point.

His name was Comanche Jim and, as the name suggested, he was a full-blooded Texas Comanche.

Besides Wick, Swede, and Gunny Rice, there was Braden who was known as *Boonie Loony,* just plain *Loony* for short. He was the guy with the tiger stripes tattooed on his face. He carried a long-bladed machete with him even on base and amused himself doing Samurai moves with it. For laughs, he'd split Spiers' cigarette in half…while he was smoking it. Class-A psycho all the way. Amoro had a Mohawk. He never spoke. He had the dead gray unblinking eyes of a reptile. He stared at Spiers constantly and when ever Spiers met his gaze, he licked his lips as if he was planning on romancing him. Another cut-throat. Then there was Weeks who was some kind of Born Again Christian who killed communists for the lord. Crockett and Garcia rounded out the team. They both had crazy eyes, but they were okay to talk to, even if Crockett claimed to be a reincarnation of Attila the Hun and Garcia—the team medic—liked to talk in great stomach-churning detail about parasitic infections.

Despite the fact that Spiers was certain he was the only sane one amongst them, he blended in fine, bending and flowing and sliding through the undergrowth with them. He was no cherry. He'd humped a ruck for eight months now. He wanted the others—Force Recon bullet-eaters and night stalkers—to see how good he was, how easy he could slip into a unit like theirs. So he moved with them, stayed with them. When they stopped, he stopped. When they pissed, he pissed. When they lay out still as decoys in the knife-grass, he laid out, too, just as quiet and smooth as steel.

But the whole time, he was thinking: *What in Jesus was I thinking, getting mixed up in this? Should've just went back home, let those shrinks pick my brain. Anything would beat the shit out of this.*

But he wasn't so sure. Maybe, deep inside, he was scared and wanted to piss a yellow stream, but outwardly, he was amped-up and he wanted a crack at this…whatever it was. If not for himself, then for Carmody. Carmody had been one of the best Marine snipers in Indochina and the fact that he let Spiers bop with him said buckets. It said he trusted him and had faith in him. An unspoken loyalty. And the way Spiers was thinking, he owed Carmody something because that loyalty went both ways.

He could almost hear that pissy jarhead now: *You damn straight you owe me, Cherry. Weren't for me they'd a bagged your green ass like bad meat day fucking one. So, get your little pecker hard, hump it, and drill that bitch what hooked my ass and drill it proper. Make it wear a ruffled pink party dress and call you fucking 'daddy.' Do it for yourself, do it for the fucking Corps, but most of all, do it for me.*

So, Spiers figured he was on a mission all his own here.

The jungle was thick and claustrophobic, the heat stifling, the air still as cream. They spent the next hour or so hiking up one forested hill and down another. And then, as dawn came on, the sun burning the mist from the landscape, the valley spread out before them and they descended into its depths, crawling down the bridges of hundred-foot fallen trees and navigating deadfalls and dips and craggy plates of rock. The jungle grew up dense and green around them to the point where they could not see one another, spread out fifteen feet apart as they were.

But finally, as the day grew hot as a skillet, the valley wall bottomed out and they found themselves in a sea of five-foot grass that was broken only by wild, knotted stands of bamboo packed tighter than bicycle spokes. It was hard going and was getting harder with each passing second.

Spiers was covered with sweat and had picked up his own personal swarm of mosquitoes that were intent on sucking him dry as a peach pit. Big, ugly mothers they were, the kind you could've roped and ridden.

He figured the team entered the valley maybe two, three klicks southeast of the point he and Carmody had weeks earlier. And maybe it was his imagination, but as soon as they started descending those forested slopes, he felt something move through him, settle inside him in a black pregnant mass. Everything seemed different—the air was heavier, the jungle more rank and decayed smelling. Breathing was like sucking air from the bottom of a rotting log. It lodged in his nostrils like cotton balls and stayed there. The odor was wrong and it made the hairs on the back of his neck stand erect.

"This the place you lost Carmody?" Wick asked him.

And Spiers could only nod. There was no mistaking it.

"But you escaped," Loony said, spitting tobacco juice into the leaves. "Ain't that just the shits? No real Marine leaves another Marine behind."

Though these guys genuinely frightened Spiers, he wasn't going to take that kind of insult. "Carmody disappeared, shit-for-brains. There wasn't anything to take back."

"Shit," Loony said.

"Big bad-ass Recon, huh? We'll see how bad-ass you are when we find that thing. When it comes for you, you'll piss your fucking pants."

Loony laughed at that…then he pulled his machete and before Spiers could do a damn thing, he had pinned him to the tree with the blade against his throat. "I suggest you watch your mouth."

"Knock it off!" Gunny Rice snapped. "I catch you playing cowboy again, Loony, and I'll shove that pig-sticker up your ass and make a pink popsicle out of you."

Loony grinned with an amazing display of bad teeth. "I got my eye on you, Spear-chucker."

Spiers watched him move out, the RPD in his arms, his body criss-crossed by ammo belts. He turned and Amoro was staring at him again. He licked his lips and blew him a kiss.

*This is fucking bullshit,* Spiers thought. *What kind of half-ass outfit is this?*

On they pushed, Comanche Jim somewhere ahead on point.

They moved into a small clearing and suddenly they could finally see each other.

Ahead, Wick raised his hand and halted the column. Comanche Jim was out in the clearing, crouched behind a low bush. Still as stone, he waited and waited.

It gave Spiers the creeps.

*Well, c'mon, let us know already. What is it? What are you seeing out there?*

Wick crept forward to join Comanche Jim. They whispered about something, then they both broke cover to look at an object that was hidden in the trees. Wick passed word down the column that he wanted Spiers forward. Spiers moved across the clearing quickly, cutting through a stand of waist-high ferns until he reached the perimeter of the green, mossy treeline.

Something was hanging from a tree limb high above, so far above its origin disappeared in the canopy. It twisted back and forth, maybe four feet off the ground. It was shriveled and gray, seamed like the bark of a dead tree. Flies buzzed around it.

Wick said, "Is this him? Is this Carmody?"

Spiers just stood there for the longest time, trembling inside, his stomach tied in a square knot. His blood had stopped flowing and his lungs had stopped breathing. Everything seemed suspended—himself, the jungle hell of Cambodia, the world at large.

Finally, his voice breaking, he said, "Yeah…that's Gunny Carmody. That's my sergeant."

He turned away then, needing a moment to himself. He wanted to rage, to shout and scream and promise the thing that haunted this valley that there would come one ugly, evil day of reckoning…but he did nothing. He already had hate in his heart. Seeing Carmody's corpse dangling there made the hate spread through his entire body until he felt like a machine with only one purpose: vengeance.

*Why?* he asked himself. *Why did I have to see this? It was bad enough without having this rubbed in my face.*

"You okay, son?" Wick asked.

"No, sir. I'm not okay at all."

Wick nodded, understanding perfectly. He'd seen friends die, he'd dragged the corpses of men who were his brothers from the jungle on numerous occasions. He knew what it felt like when that bond was broken by death. He knew it only too well.

"Well, we better cut him down," Wick said, motioning some of the others forward. "We owe him that much."

*I owe him a lot more,* Spiers thought.

"That wire he's hanging from," he said. "We saw some of it that day we were here. It's strong. Carmody thought it might be some kind of synthetic."

But nobody was believing that.

They knew it wasn't man-made.

Swede and Weeks handled the mummy of Carmody carefully, as if it might break apart in their hands. They took hold of the legs, then the web belt around his waist and pulled down on it. They were trying to snap the white thread that held him but it proved to be remarkably elastic like a rubber band. They could pull Carmody all the way to the ground so that his boots were touching, but if they released him, up he went again. Gunny Rice ordered Loony and Amoro into the act and along with Swede and Weeks, they all pulled down on Carmody. While they did that, Comanche Jim used the saw edge of his fighting knife to cut through it.

It wasn't easy.

It took him a good ten or twenty seconds of exertion to cut the strand. When he did, Carmody dropped into the arms of the others and the strand snapped back up into the misty treetops before floating back down, drifting on a column of air, sort of gauzy and ethereal.

Wick sawed a section of it from Carmody and tucked it gently into a plastic map pouch. Spiers knew it wasn't for the hell of it; somebody back at command wanted this stuff, probably to see if their scientists could duplicate it.

In the heat of the jungle, Spiers, Swede, and Garcia dug a shallow grave and placed the mummy of Carmody into it, burying it quickly and spreading leaves and loam about so the ground cover looked undisturbed.

"Rest easy, Gunny Carmody," Wick said, giving Spiers' shoulder a pat. "Your day of reckoning is swiftly approaching."

# 17

Comanche Jim moved out on point and the column followed suit, Loony and Weeks fanning out to the flank. The farther they moved into the primeval hell of the valley, the more eerie the atmosphere became. It was no one thing. The shadows seemed to be thicker, the undergrowth more wiry and tangled, vines and flowering creepers dangling from tree limbs overhead like green tentacles. Ground mist seeped from the earth. There were immense fleshy orchids that were bloated dead white like the bellies of corpses. Earlier, the jungle had been a hive of cawing and shrilling and droning, now it was dead silent. There was no sound save a weak, listless breeze in the treetops overhead. Spiers was very much aware of it. He was also aware that he was feeling what he felt upon originally entering the valley—the sense of being watched, scrutinized.

It made his skin crawl.

They moved into a clearing with Comanche Jim. Though it was a dangerous break in unit discipline—a VC ambush could've cut half of them down with ease—Wick didn't seem to mind. But then, he wasn't worrying about anything human.

Not here.

Comanche Jim squatted there, studying the trees. "There's…there's something out there, Major. Something watching us."

"What?"

Comanche Jim shook his head side to side. "I don't know…but it's boocoo bad."

Sweat dripping from the end of his nose, Spiers licked his lips and listened to his heart play "Taps." Comanche Jim was real good. A natural. Creepier than a bag of spiders, but very good. Guy didn't seem to sweat. Spiers couldn't imagine anyone or anything that could have spooked him, but something had.

"It's gone," Comanche Jim said. "Like it never was."

The team started breathing again and Wick got them moving after taking a compass reading.

They chopped through thick undergrowth and marched through flaxen grass into a green swamp. The muddy brown water reached up past their knees and finally to their waists and they had to move real slowly to avoid the twisted, reaching roots of trees growing up out of it. It was a tangled, watery mess and it reminded Spiers of the mangrove swamps down in the Delta. It was foggy and dim in there, the foliage overhead blocking out all but a few gloomy fingers of sunlight. Hundreds of bats roosted above, squeaking and chirping and dropping gray clots of shit on the Marines. Now and then, a swarm would light into the air, diving and dipping over their heads. Gradually, the canopy above completely blotted out the feeble light and the world became grim and shadowy, pooling with blackness and stifling, damp heat. Leeches dropped from leaves and slithered in the water. Unseen things moved and splashed and swam. There were snakes and giant dragonflies and lizards and little birds caught in spreading spider webs.

They finally made it out after a few hour's hike through one of the most inhospitable and dangerous ecosystems on earth.

Then the sun was on them and it felt good, but the air was still torpid and stagnant. And right away, just inside a congested stand of triple-canopy jungle, Comanche Jim stopped. The others moved up on him.

He didn't seem afraid this time, just perplexed. "Major," he said. "There's something ahead. Up in that fucking tree."

Ahead of them was a deadfall of trees that had collapsed into one another as if some raging storm had swept through there. In the center of that jumble of snaking limbs, matted foliage, and dense curtains of hanging moss, there was a stout teak that rose up into the canopy above. It was wide and massive at its base, becoming slender as it shot up through the leafage. Up maybe twenty feet, there was something white snarled in a nest of snaking offshoots and gnarled branches. It was hard to say what it was, but it surely wasn't a natural object.

Spiers was thinking parachute canvas…but even that didn't seem to fit.

Wick pulled off his bush hat, wiped sweat from his black-streaked brow. "Swede? Take Spiers with you. Go see what it is."

They dropped their packs, unsheathed their machetes and started scaling the rampart of logs and dead trees like monkeys while Loony and Amoro covered them with the RPDs. It was hard going, treacherous going. The bark was wet and rotting and hard to get a footing on, the moss so thick it had to be cut through. Spiers followed Swede, avoiding a limb upon which a ten-foot python was coiling.

Carefully, slowly, they neared the white mass.

Water dripped from the leaves overhead and spiders the size of mice skittered over the network of branches. Spiers and Swede ducked under boughs and snaked over limbs and finally, they were on it.

"Fuck is that?" Spiers said.

Swede just shook his head, stroking the drooping tips of his mustache. "I don't know," he whispered.

It was maybe four or five feet long with the general girth of a roll of carpet and seemed to be made of the same white, stringy material that Carmody had hung from. But this was a woven, intricate mass. It looked—if anything—like a big cocoon. Strands and streamers of the stuff fastened it between the teak and a few dead branches.

Swede cut it loose, sawing through the anchor lines with a lot of sweating and grunting. The mass fell, end over end, to the ground below, busting a hole through the greenage and crashing into the undergrowth.

By the time they made it back to the ground, the others were standing around it like mourners over a grave. Something had burst through the material—a human hand. Gray fingers like mummified twigs jutted in the air.

Wick took out his knife and slit it open like a pea pod, half-cutting and half-sawing. The body in there was curled and fissured and drawn up into a fetal position. There was no way to tell its race or gender such was the degree of morbid dissolution.

"Looks…looks like something cocooned it up in there," Comanche Jim said, his voice low and concerned. "Sucked it dry."

"That's crazy," Rice said, trying to remain rational. "Ain't no bug big enough to do that."

But Comanche Jim was laughing. A great booming sound that echoed through that sullen jungle. But it was not a laughter of mirth or good cheer, but a maddened cackling that was equal parts anger and disbelief. "Don't you get it?" he said, stalking around in a circle now, hands held up to the sky. "That thing…it catches men like a spider catches flies! It webs them up and drains the juice out of 'em a little at a time!"

He kept laughing, but no one else thought it was funny.

Not in the least.

Even Loony and Amoro looked nervous.

Comanche Jim was giving everyone the willies so Gunny Rice told him to knock it the hell off and act like a Marine and not a schoolboy. He had no more finished dressing him down when there was a sound of movement out in the jungle.

"Hell is that?" Swede whispered.

But no one knew.

Not for sure.

Something was out there. Something *big*. It was a huge crashing sound as if some immense beast was circling them in the jungle. Dead trees were falling and crashing, limbs snapping free, sticks crunching. Whatever in the hell it was, it must have had great weight. They could hear the sucking sounds of it pulling its feet from the mucky, spongy ground.

His guts pulling up tight as bedsprings, Spiers waited there with the others, his fingers sweating on his MAT-49. Every muscle in his body was knotted tight. Sweat ran down his face and insects buzzed at his ears.

An odor came out of the jungle that reminded him of wet animal hides, it was thick and sickening. It grew strong enough so that a gag reflex made him cough quietly. The creature continued to move around in the jungle as if it were searching for something, getting closer and closer, the stench of rotting pelts nearly unbearable.

Then it stopped.

The jungle was quiet.

Nobody moved. They didn't even breathe.

They waited there listening for ten more minutes but there were no more sounds. Whatever it was, it was either silently lying in wait or it had vanished. Even the smell was gone. Nobody commented on it. The very idea of putting something like that into words was simply unthinkable.

They moved back into the jungle, hacking their way forward and Comanche Jim found some prints in the loam. They were immense. It looked like pillars had been slammed down into the forest floor, dozens of them. The holes were each two feet deep and over a foot across. This was the spoor of the thing they had heard. Its path ahead was clear—a huge hole cut through the jungle by something which must have been the size of a tractor-trailer.

Thankfully, it moved off in the opposite direction.

The landscape began to get hilly and it was just like being in the Highlands again, up one hill and down another. Whenever they paused atop one, all they could see were more green hills stretching away into the haze. They looked like tropical islands rising from a sea of mist.

After a time, the hills seemed to play out and they were on level ground again, threading their way around black sucking bogs and deadfalls draped with mossy creepers. They were getting closer to something and they all felt it deep inside, like a knife blade scraping along the inside of their skulls. They kept hearing sounds out in the forest—big sounds—but Wick and Gunny Rice kept them moving because, as they said, they weren't on a nature hike here.

About a half hour later, Crockett was on point in the sweltering heat, moving quickly and carefully and low over the muddy ground. He stepped easily over a rotting log, avoiding a large poisonous centipede, and stepped between two trees.

Spiers, at the head of the column with Wick, saw it happen.

Crockett stepped between two trees and then he screamed as if he had been pierced by a lance. They saw him there, fighting and twisting. Spiers and the others rushed forward and saw that he was caught in a net of the white filaments that was stretched between the two trees like some sort of crazy spider web. The more he fought, the more tangled he became.

By the time Wick and Spiers got to him, he was pretty thoroughly wrapped in the stuff and the perfectly horrifying thing about it was that it didn't seem to be just his panic and thrashing that was causing it. The webs were *moving*. There was no doubt of it. They were sliding over him, winding him up like lariats, noosing and constricting. A strand had encircled his throat and it was tightening fast, his breath barely coming, his face going a violent shade of purple.

"Gahhhhh," he gasped. *"Gggghhhhh..."*

Though most were shocked into inaction, Wick waded right in, taking hold of the strand that held his throat and slicing through it so he could breathe. Then Swede and Comanche Jim and Gunny Rice got into the act followed by Spiers. The web filaments were more like cords and had the general thickness of piano wires. They all began sawing through them. Spiers took hold of a strand that had wound itself around Crockett's waist. It moved in his hands like an angry snake. He cut into it with his knife and it was like trying to saw through glass. But that was just the tough outer membrane. Once he got through it, the strand trembled in his hands as if it were writhing in pain. He cut deeper and it opened like a severed artery, pale green goo squirting across the back of his hand and bringing a stinging sort of pain.

*Bleeding,* he thought with rising madness. *It's fucking bleeding.*

The others were experiencing the same thing and as they cut and slashed and tried to free Crockett—who was nearly out of his mind with terror as the filaments crept over him like worms—there was a high-pitched shrilling noise from high, high above them. It sounded like a cry of agony.

The strands loosened.

They dropped Crockett to the ground and began to retreat up into the trees. Spiers saw this at the same moment that he saw two or three gray spiders crawling over the downed man. He swatted one of them away and it exploded with a gushing of gray-black slime. They weren't spiders exactly, but oval-bodied things more like ticks with bodies the size of tennis balls and a multitude of skittering, stubby legs.

*Disgusting,* is what he thought.

They dragged Crockett into the jungle and set up a defensive perimeter while Garcia salved burns and abrasions and gave Crockett a good going over. There seemed to be nothing physically wrong with him other than the fact he had the shakes and he kept scratching and pawing at his body as if he could still feel the gray ticks crawling over him. The black-and-green camo paint on his face had been worn off in places and the skin beneath was of an unhealthy yellow hue. His eyes were wide and stark. He looked absolutely petrified, practically hysterical with terror.

"Things," he muttered in a voice dry as rust. "Things all over me...*crawling all over me...they're all over me!*"

"Quiet him the fuck down," Wick snapped. They were on an operation here; there was no room for weak nerves and hysterics.

"Easy," Spiers told him. "We got them off you. It's okay now."

Crockett had been struggling, but slowly he relaxed and lay there, breathing in and out. His eyes stared up into the trees. "It happened," he said in a low voice. "It really happened."

"You were caught, but we got you out," Garcia told him.

His head whipped back and forth. "No, no...not that. Not that." He swallowed a few times, licking his lips repeatedly. "While I was in that...that fucking web and those things were crawling on me, wrapping me tighter...I saw things."

"Hell is he yammering about?" Gunny Rice wanted to know.

Crockett's eyes swam in their sockets. He offered Spiers a sallow, nervous grin. *"I saw things,"* he whispered. "I really *saw* things."

"What kind of things?" Garcia asked.

A huge fly had settled on Crockett's cheek and was investigating his left nostril. He seemed completely unaware of it. "Up there," he said. "Up above. I could see things from high up above like *I* was up in the trees looking down at us. I did. I really did."

"He's fucking hallucinating," Rice said.

But Spiers didn't think so. Crockett definitely wasn't in his right state of mind, but there was something very lucid about what he was saying. "Up above...up *there*. I was looking down. Looking down at us. I could see me in the web and...and...and *it made me hungry.*"

"Jesus Christ. He lost his mind," someone said.

Again, Spiers didn't think so. Wick and Swede and some of the others had drawn in closer now and he could see by the look in their eyes that they did not believe Crockett had gone crazy.

"When you guys cut me loose," he said, "it…it *hurt! It was like you were cutting into me! I could feel the pain of the thing up there…it was angry!"*

"He's gone head-over-heels bugfuck," Rice said. "That's the last thing we need out here."

"You gotta get your shit together," Wick told him. "We can't afford this and we don't have the time for it. Whatever happened is over. Now I'm giving you a direct order—proceed with mission, proceed to objective. Do I make myself clear?"

Whether it was his rigorous training or the self-discipline of a Marine, Crockett climbed shakily to his feet. He was still scared. He was still out of his head. But he knew better than to compromise a mission. Spiers had the worst feeling that if he hadn't snapped out of it, Wick would have killed him.

Comanche Jim took point and the team was on the move again, everyone watching for those webs now. This operation had been deadly serious before and now it had taken on a whole new dimension. This forest was haunted by something that was beyond imagination.

And the farther they went, the longer the shadows grew, the darker the jungle, and the more unearthly the atmosphere.

# 18

They moved forward another thirty minutes and things gradually got worse.

The jungle grew heavier, if such a thing were possible, more twisted and clotted with creepers and hanging vines and bamboo reeds. Insects droned and ants crawled and huge spiders skittered up the mossy trunks of immense swamp cypress trees. It was a world of hot green stagnation like something straight out of the Paleozoic. Now and then they could swear they heard something up above, slipping through the treetops. And in the trees themselves, more of those cocoons were strung up like fishing nets.

Spiers was dreaming, fantasizing really, of some military psych ward back in the States, because, Jesus, it had to have been better than this. At least the insanity there was contained. Here it was given full rein; it had found fertile ground and blossomed in the dank, black soil.

It was…it was like unhallowed ground, he thought. The sight of atrocities and mayhem so vile the human brain could not hope, nor dare, to fathom. The atmosphere was physically suffocating, humid, rank, fetid, and spiritually noxious. It hung over the team like a wormy shroud, draped over them, filling their hearts with a foul black sap and their souls with something putrid.

Spiers had known fear before. He'd lived with it for months now.

But this was just plain bad, even worse than the nights in that POW camp. It was huge and horrid, filling his belly in sickening waves and making something wither and die deep inside him. Menace seemed to ooze and trickle from the jungle and that silence, that immense and blanketing silence, seemed to scream, to thrum in the air.

They would die here, the lot of them, he decided with an unpleasant certainty that was neither terrifying nor disquieting, but simply a fact. Die here in this stagnant, rotting green hell, the life sucked from them and their bones going to powder in the sluicing gray mud.

The air was grainy and moist and hard to breathe. You could feel it on your teeth like ash blown from an urn. The vegetation was thick and crawling with some malignant life, but there was no sign of animals. It was like shambling through the dark bowels of some gigantic haunted house, and to a man, the Marines were scared shitless. They'd been in other nasty stretches of wilderness in that war, but nothing could touch the atmosphere of this place. So silent, so decayed, so filled with…death. And quiet. Graveyard quiet. No birds, no monkeys, no insects. Nothing. Sterile and antiseptic like some laboratory hothouse.

They were packed closer together, not giving a good goddamn about ambushes now. They needed the closeness of one another, the companionship of living, breathing human beings and not those embalmed, gruesome things dangling from the trees. They were seeing dozens of them now—huge mummy-shaped cocoons hanging from tree limbs high above on white threads like puppets.

And all Spiers could think about was Crockett and that crazy shit about him being able to see through the eyes of some thing watching them from high above, feeling its hunger and pain. It was madness. Sheer madness. As if being in that web had given him some psychic link with it.

Some of the others were muttering to themselves and making weird, choking sounds in their throats as if they were fighting back tears or screams.

Spiers wanted to cry out himself, to run blindly through the malefic jungle. But if he did, if he found himself alone in those stygian, spectral depths, he would have no choice but to put the barrel of his weapon in his mouth and blow his brains to sauce.

"Quiet and keep moving," Wick told them when they began to cluster together, when they probed into black, festering thickets, when the shadows grew long and sharp and things seemed to move and prance just out of sight.

It was more than just the cocooned bodies now, for those webs were everywhere.

They were tangled in the grasses, fanning out over the undergrowth. Winding sheets of them reached from branches above to the ground and were snared between the trunks of trees. Limbs were braided with them and the high canopy meshed in transparent blankets.

They had to chop through them with their machetes.

Once, as he hacked and cut, Spiers felt one of them brush the back of his hand and he cried out. For it did not feel like web, but warm and pulsing like something alive, a living flypaper.

*Alive?* he wondered feverishly. *Alive? Yes, some of those webs are alive and some are nothing but webs. But how do you tell? How do you know? How do you really distinguish between them?*

There was no way to know. Not really. This entire operation was taking on the patterns of a nightmare and real-world logic did not seem to apply. Nothing could surprise him in this place. He sensed danger around them, above them. There were whickering, rustling sounds off in the jungle to all sides and he did not want to know what was making them. He had the most awful feeling that if he saw them, he would go mad.

Comanche Jim came back in for a quick consult with Major Wick. Their faces were grim indeed in the patchy sunlight filtering through the thick canopy above. Wick passed something to Gunny Rice and Rice formed the team into a wagon wheel defensive perimeter.

"Whatever's out there," he said. "It's closing in from all sides."

They could all hear it.

The truly scary part was that it was not just from the tangled dark thickets of jungle around them or leaning stands of bamboo, but from above. Things rustled and lurked. A sharp, pungent odor seemed to be coming through the dense foliage. It smelled like old varnish or embalming fluid…positively acrid and unnatural.

The men waited with fingers on triggers, sweat running down the smeared camo paint on their faces. Eyes were wide and hearts were drumming. This was the very worst part: the waiting. Once contact came and the fighting began, all the bad nervous energy and anxiety could be purged, but until that moment these things ran wild in each man. And particularly because they had no idea what was going to come out of the jungle at them.

Spiers waited there, wanting to shoot, needing a target, but there was nothing. Only the sounds of things circling around them, quick creeping forms. Black phantom shapes that were there and then gone just as fast.

The smell increased.

Several of the Marines made gagging sounds.

Spiers knew damn well that what they were about to face was not human. Even if it hadn't been for the things he had seen in that terrible valley thus far, he would have known this because whatever was out there did not move like men—it crept, it skittered, it stalked with a fluid multi-legged grace.

The jungle was dead silent.

No birds calling or insects buzzing. The primordial green hell of the valley seemed as if it was holding its breath. That smell seemed to gather around them in toxic clouds, saturating the perimeter like poison gas, growing stronger until it was oddly sweet like the inside of a honeycomb. And before anyone dared comment on the freakish nature of such a thing, they heard a series of strident cries out in the jungle. They were quick, shrilling *sssskrrreeeeek!* sort of sounds, like insects and possibly more specific, grasshoppers. They came from every direction, a chain of them winding off in the forest until they could barely be heard.

Spiers, of course, had heard it before, the last time he was in the valley. He knew damn well the things were communicating in their harsh, piercing voices, gathering to attack or ambush the intruders or hatch some equally nefarious plot. Whatever they were, they were certainly not unintelligent. They were organized and, he thought, they seemed to operate in a cooperative, unified manner like a tribe…or an army.

*Any second now, any fucking second now,* a voice in his head warned him. *Something's going to happen. Something very bad.*

"Do not break formation for any reason," Wick told them. "You see a target, take it out."

Spiers knew damn well that in a conventional infantry unit that would have been carte blanche for everyone to start opening up, pulverizing the foliage with sustained fire, but the Recon Marines were too self-disciplined for that. They were not going to shoot at shadows or imaginary forms. They would not waste a single round until that round had a definite target.

As a sniper, Spiers scanned his sector of jungle with a practiced eye. He had spent the past eight months trying to ferret out the difference between hidden enemies and innocuous forms that only *looked* like the enemy such as bushes, palm fronds, and crouching ferns. He was not easily fooled. Like Swede, he had put away his MAT-49 submachine gun and swapped it for the Dragunov sniper rifle. Long-distance shooting would be important now.

Using the scope, he studied the terrain carefully, his heart pounding and sweat droplets running down his face like tears. Ahead was relatively open ground, rugged and filled with dips and draws, jutting green-slimed tree roots and rotting logs. It was shaded by huge ferns and set with sucking black pools of standing water that were probably alive with snakes, slugs, and leeches as well as microscopic terrors like amoebas and liver flukes. Beyond that, there was a stand of waist-deep elephant grass for maybe thirty feet or so. It was nearly impenetrable, at least for anything that walked upright like a man. Then the real jungle started, a heavy clustering run of trees and vines and leafy brush.

The rustling sounds continued.

Something was in the elephant grass. It was gliding confidently through it at ground level. There were a few more screeching cries from the jungle answered by irregular high-pitched peeping noises in the grass.

Spiers knew everyone wanted to shoot as badly as he did. *Target, target, target.* That's what it was all about. He was studying a black shape that seemed to be skulking about a fallen stand of dead trees. It could have been a shadow. It could have been nothing at all, but his finely honed instinct told him that it was a living, animate thing that was watching them, pretending to be nothing at all.

It was at the very edge of the elephant grass.

He sighted in on it.

He didn't want to be the first one to open up, but he knew that Major Wick was counting on him and Swede to find the encroaching enemy before they got too close.

He scanned around the black shape out there. Was it or wasn't it? There was only one way to find out. He locked the crosshairs on it, sucked in a breath, and let it out slowly through his teeth.

He squeezed the trigger and the rifle cracked.

His round hit the shape and it stumbled back into the jungle, letting out an eerie inhuman cry. Whatever it was, it was alive. Swede fired seconds after he did, hitting two more shapes out there. One of them made a short screeching sound and the other wailed into the jungle, sounding very much like a woman screaming hysterically.

"LIGHT UP THAT GRASS!" Wick ordered.

Rounds were concentrated into the elephant grass. Grenades were fired into its depths, fragmentation and incendiary. It burned, it flaked, it collapsed beneath the churning smoke of white phosphorus. The grass erupted with explosions of flying earth as the frags tore it apart and the incendiaries lit it up. It exploded, drifting in the air in fragments. Things cried out in there, rising from the inferno, pulverized in interlocking fields of fire from the Marines and going back down. The air was filled with smoke and debris. No one could say what they were shooting at…only that it was fast and horrible and had too many legs. They all died with the same hypersonic keening sounds.

Whatever was massing out there, pulled back.

"CEASE FIRE!" Wick called out.

It was chaos and confusion now with the grass blazing away, smoke blowing in the air, hanging over the ground like clouds of morning mist. If something was trying to get in at them, now would have been the time. The smoke was the perfect camouflage.

"Listen," Comanche Jim said.

*Oh Christ, not again, not again,* Spiers thought.

That immense thing that they'd heard before was coming back again. And this time, it was coming right at them. It was moving through the jungle behind them. They could hear the underbrush cracking, more trees falling, the steady booming of its footsteps. Spiers felt cold sweat run down the back of his neck as he heard these things and thought of the immense holes in the ground the creature's tread had left behind.

And now it was coming at them.

If they waited another five minutes or so, it would push itself out of the jungle and they'd see what it was and Spiers didn't think that would be a good idea at all.

"You know what that is?" Loony asked Spiers. "It's Death. And it's coming for you. And I get to watch it take you."

Spiers forced a laugh. "And I get to see you piss your pants."

"We better get out of here," Swede said.

He got no arguments. Major Wick took out his maps and had a quick word or two with Gunny Rice. The ground was shaking with the monstrous tread of the beast. Branches and leaves fell from nearby trees, the jungle crashing and splitting as that horror pushed forward. Spiers could smell its foul stench pushing out of the forest in hot, rank waves again—rotting hides and wormy pelts, skins decayed and threadbare.

*Enough.*

"All right," Wick said. "We're going to continue mission. Weeks? You got the point. Lead us on out."

By then, Spiers could hear trees—really *big* trees—falling over like dominoes. The jarring of the beast's tread made the ground vibrate like a low-level quake was shaking things up.

Weeks cut away from the burning grass field and scouted his way into the jungle and the team followed, Braden taking up the back door, casting fearful looks behind him.

# 19

Weeks led them deeper into the primordial rain forest of the valley floor. Gnarled trees rose hundreds of feet above, their branches fanning out into a lush green triple canopy that let only a few misty, struggling beams of sunlight through. Their trunks were green with moss and sprouted immense parasitic colonies of toadstools. Green vines hung down in a mass profusion like hundreds of emerald ropes. The ground was littered with dead leaves, bunched creepers, snakelike roots, and spreading fetid pools of black water teeming with leeches and clouds of mosquitoes. Snakes slid through the underbrush and small foraging mammals sought cover as the team moved ever forward to their destination.

Spiers figured that only Wick and Rice knew where that was.

And at that moment, he, like the others, had other things to worry about.

That creature—that gargantuan *thing*—was still following them. It wasn't moving fast, but it *was* moving. And the closer it got, the more they began to hear a weird crackling/grinding sort of sound that reminded Spiers oddly enough of meshing gears locking and unlocking. What he would have given at that moment for something ordinary like an ambush. Something real. Something tangible. Something he could have fought against. The creature was beyond anything he could imagine. It was like some immense force of nature. Thunder. Lightning. Storm winds. Earthquakes. A relentless elemental wrath.

He had overheard a few conversations between Gunny Rice and Major Wick. From the gist of it, he knew they were worried. Had the team been back over the fence in Vietnam and in range of a firebase, they would have called an artillery strike down on it. An air strike even. But for now, there was only escape and evasion until they reached their target.

Behind them, in the forest the thing approached, knocking over trees and cutting a swath through the jungle.

When the line of march paused so that Wick could take some compass readings, Loony said, "You want my opinion? We wait for it, then we pour everything we got at it. A big game hunt."

Amoro just nodded. Weeks and Garcia seemed to like the idea as well. They were tired of running. Tired of trying to escape this goddamn phantom. They wanted to fight it out.

Comanche Jim laughed, burning leeches off himself with a cigarette. "You want my opinion, Loony? Your opinion sucks ass."

Swede giggled.

"And why's that?" Loony had to ask.

"Because it's suicide," Comanche Jim told him. "That thing is a good mile behind us and the ground is shaking and we can hear the forest being laid flat. You want to come up against something like that with these pea shooters?" He held up his MAT-49. "It would be like throwing a handful of rice at it. You can't kill a tornado with a slingshot."

"Davey killed Goliath with a slingshot," Weeks said. "It was in the Bible."

"That was a fable, numbnuts," Rice said. "It was a fairy tale. In reality, Goliath stepped on Davey and laughed when Davey's guts squirted out of his mouth."

Weeks, who considered himself some kind of Bible thumper, tried to defend his position but no one was listening. They had more pressing concerns. The most serious of which was the thing that just kept coming and coming.

Spiers joined Wick and Comanche Jim on a hilltop. Wick handed him his spotting scope. "Look," he said.

Spiers did and wished that he hadn't. He saw several trees far in the distance fall one by one. Whatever was causing it was lost in the haze, but for a second there he caught sight of some gigantic slate-gray wall pushing forward, moving with a lurching, creeping sort of motion…then it was lost to view. He could still smell the creature and he could hear that grinding sound echoing through the valley. There was another sound just underneath it, a sort of low constant humming or droning. It was steady, perpetual. For a second, he thought he saw the gray shape again and this time it looked like bolts of lightning were arcing from it.

Then it was gone again.

Rice went down the hill and got the others up and ready to move. Crockett was in a bad way. Swede had to help him to his feet. His knees were tottering and when he stood, slumped-over, his face was pale and mottled, eyes like warm glass. He rarely spoke. He was now a detriment to the operation and Spiers knew it.

"What are we gonna do with him, sir?" Spiers asked Wick.

"I don't know, son. If this was an ordinary patrol, we'd probably have to leave him and swing back for him later. But with that…that *animal* coming, we can't be leaving men, now can we?"

"No, we can't."

Down the hill, the Recon Marines were all looking spooked, all acting strange (even for them). Weeks was praying under his breath. Loony was whispering to his machete. Comanche Jim was smiling, sensing something in the treetops no one else could. Gunny Rice stood over them, looking pissed off. The ground continued to shake. That grinding/crackling sound grew louder and louder. Which was bad enough, but it was the constant background droning noise that bothered Spiers the most. It grated his nerves. It made his teeth ache. It reminded him of power lines humming at mid-summer.

Swede and Garcia were tending to Crockett, who was mumbling nonsensical things under his breath.

Spiers went over to him. "How you holding up?" he asked, even though he knew it was an unbelievably stupid thing to ask.

"It'll keep coming," Crockett said. "That's what it's supposed to do. Keep coming and coming."

"What is it?"

Crockett couldn't tell him that. Whoever he had been before, he was someone else now. He was broken, the heart taken out of him, his soul removed and replaced by a black sucking emptiness. His eyes were filled with tears and they splashed down his cheeks. Whatever had happened to him in that web, he was ruined now.

The crackling and grinding sounds were getting much louder and everyone was aware of it. Spiers knew that these men were frightened. Frightened because they were used to be being the big bad boogeymen of the jungle. *Swift, silent, deadly.* That was their motto. They came in the night like ghosts and you never knew they were there. Now instead of being the hunters, they were being hunted and they really didn't know how to react to it. Psychologically, it was devastating.

"Let's get the fuck out of here," Wick said.

# 20

Whatever the hell that thing was, they lost it about twenty minutes later. As before, they just stopped hearing it as if it had stepped off this world and into another. There, then gone. Every man was near-hysterical with mounting fear, the fear of prey, and then the sounds were gone and they were left wondering if they had heard them at all.

Spiers knew better, of course, as he figured all the others did. Whatever that thing was, it was out there, and any time it chose, it would return.

*It'll keep coming. That's what it's supposed to do. Keep coming and coming.*

Crockett's words. Spiers didn't know how he knew that, but he believed him.

For the next thirty minutes, all was calm. They heard nothing and saw no weird webs or mummies in the trees and was that a good sign or a bad sign? Wick kept referring to his maps, but as Swede pointed out, this place had never been mapped out before. What they had was based on aerial reconnaissance, so it was anyone's guess if they were even moving in the right direction of the target. Yet, Wick seemed very confident in all he did and Spiers could not imagine a guy like him getting them lost or leading them on a wild goose chase (much as such an idea might be a relief).

They'd been on the march for some time by then and Rice let them have ten minutes to get off their feet. They spread out in a wagon wheel defensive perimeter and ate a few C-rations and smoked a few cigarettes. Nobody spoke. They were too busy listening.

Spiers was glad when Rice got them moving again. Just waiting like that made him feel more like a target than ever.

Comanche Jim was back on point, sliding through the jungle like a viper, smooth, easy, and sinuous. He moved quickly yet carefully and amazingly silent.

The cobwebs—because that's exactly what they looked like—were not sporadic in the vegetation now but seemingly everywhere. The Marines were in a forest of them. Thick interwoven plaits of them grew from the trees like angel hair, spreading from branch to branch to branch, engulfing entire trunks and limbs, growing from high above, stretched tight by anchor strands attached to deadfalls and stumps and logs on the forest floor. The weak sunbeams shining through them were a dirty jaundiced yellow like light coming through stained glass.

Everyone stepped carefully, avoiding fibers and ropes of webs and great nets that shivered between leaning boles.

It made Spiers' flesh crawl.

He was reminded of how the apple trees had looked back home one summer when tent caterpillars had invaded, spinning great white cottony cocoons amongst the branches and making the orchard look as if it had been infested with spiders. It looked very much like that, only more profuse and busy and on an immense scale.

Comanche Jim crept back to the column and told Wick that there was movement ahead. Whoever—or whatever—was coming, they were coming in numbers.

Wick had them pull back, clearing the webworks as much as possible and getting a thick stand of bamboo at their backs as they established a perimeter on a low hilltop with clear kill zones in all directions. Loony and Amoro set up their RPDs at the left and right flanks and Rice wired four Claymore mines together in the underbrush. If the enemy came in numbers, he'd fire them simultaneously with a single clacker.

Then, everyone in position, they waited.

The jungle dripped and birds cawed, insects buzzed around them, chiggers and mosquitoes nipping at their necks. They were hearing sounds out there, not the big sounds of the beast but the small rustlings of men pushing through the undergrowth with little or no attempt at stealth.

Both Swede and Spiers were watching the jungle through the scopes of their sniper rifles, Wick and Rice were doing the same with their spotting scopes.

The rustling continued.

Then, through that fog of webs, a dozen figures and then a dozen more drifted out at them like ghosts. Here was what they had been waiting for, what they all secretly needed, a way to purge their frustrations and fears and anxiety.

"Hold fire until my signal," Wick said.

He wanted to get the enemy in close and grease them all at once. No sense wasting ammunition when it could—hopefully—be taken care of in a few seconds of sustained firing.

Like the others, Spiers waited, sighting targets with his Dragunov. His MAT-49 lay in the grass next to him, several frag grenades close at hand with their pins straightened. The others were doing the same, arranging their killing hardware so it would be ready when the time came.

The figures looked like VC irregulars in their tattered black fatigues. They carried AKs and Russian semi-autos and Chinese machine pistols. They stumbled forward with glazed eyes, filthy and haggard, more like living skeletons than soldiers. Strands of web were snarled on the barrels of their rifles and stuck to their chests and spread over their faces like cauls. By then, there were easily fifty of them.

"Snipers," Wick said. "Waste 'em."

Swede fired first.

He dropped two VC at long-rang and Spiers popped three of them. In an average combat scenario, this would have gotten the other VC scrambling for cover, but it had no effect on them. They came on, stumbling forward, firing their weapons blindly with no real targets, just squeezing the triggers until their magazines were empty. Some of them kept squeezing them long afterwards.

Wick still told everyone to hold their fire, letting Spiers and Swede indiscriminately drop enemy soldiers with their sniper rifles. Then when the surviving VC were up close and personal, clustered together in a knot, maybe twenty or thirty of them, Rice fired the Claymores. Each one contained 700 ball bearings encased in a shaped charge of C-4. The detonation was jarring. When the smoke cleared, there was nothing but gore and body parts sprayed for fifty feet in every direction.

But more of the enemy were coming.

Then everyone was shooting and there was the popping of MATs and the rattle of the 56 rifles and the dull thuds of shotguns. Grenades were exploding and men were crying out and the Marines with the RPDs were spraying down the jungle. The VC came on, taking dozens of rounds before going down. Some of them came on with their heads blown to pulp and their faces blasted to raw meat. They were open and bleeding and sometimes had no arms and trailed intestines, but they refused to die easily.

More of them stormed forward and the fighting was close-in and bloody, the Marines peppered with the gore of the enemy. One of them emptied an entire magazine from his submachine gun into a VC and still he came on, his hide punched with countless holes. Weeks hammered his head open with the butt of his SMG and, avoiding three others, jumped through the ferns for a direct assault and ran straight into a screen of webs that held him like a housefly as he screamed and fought.

Seconds later, he was just…gone.

A VC leaped on Spiers, kicking his rifle out of his hands, and Spiers managed to flip him over and get his knife out. He slid it into the thrashing VC's throat and slit open his windpipe and jugular in one stroke, but blood burst into his eyes, blinding him. He pushed the body aside and wiped his face clean.

*I'll never get it all off me,* he thought then. *I'll never wash all this blood off me.*

But he shook that from his mind because he knew the sort of weird phobias that could develop from thinking that way. Sometimes grunts that saw a lot of action and did a lot of killing of the close-in variety would get a bad case of the heebie-jeebies from all the blood and pretty soon it was a full-blown psychosis that they couldn't shake. They'd see blood on their hands when there wasn't any, feel it dripping down their faces, and smell it on themselves no matter how much showering, soaping, and scrubbing they did back at the base. Once that started, they were no good. They needed psychiatric help.

The VC he had killed—looked like a fifteen-year-old kid—was starting to move.

Spiers blinked his eyes two or three times to force the vision from his head but it wouldn't go away. *You're losing it. You know you're fucking losing it.* But he began to believe otherwise because that body was *really* moving.

He looked over at Swede and the others, wanting to say, *you see this, you see this shit?* but they were involved in loading their weapons and arranging their gear in case more unfriendlies decided to crash the party.

The body moved again.

There was no way it could, not with its throat slit wide open like that and all of its blood soaking into the soil. It couldn't possibly be. But it *was.* There was no mistaking it; the body was moving with a sort of slow, jerking motion the way bait will as it floats atop a summer pond, something hitting it from below.

*Am I really fucking seeing this?*

No one else had noticed, not just yet. Spiers could notice nothing else. He had tunnel vision. Had a dozen NVA shithoppers come charging out of the brush with AKs blazing, they would have been promptly ignored. His perception had narrowed to an acute sharpness like the tip of a pin.

The body moved again, then again with that same jerking motion and he was unaware of the fact that he was flinching each time it did so. Its slit throat was like a second grinning mouth.

Spiers just watched, trembling now from head to toe. Sweat that was hot and foul-smelling ran down his face. His vision seemed to blur. His head swam with a swooning, hysterical sort of terror and he had to bite down on his lower lip so he did not cry out.

*Look, look, look,* a voice chanted in his head. *Do you see it? Do you see it? Do you see it?*

The blood-spattered face of the corpse was turned in his direction, one eye open and bleary, the other closed, its mouth grinning in a death rictus. Every time the body moved, the grin seemed to get a little bit wider until the entire face became a mocking and horribly sardonic mask, the smiling sewn-on face of a rag doll.

Spiers wanted to look away, but he didn't dare. The heat. The humidity. This accursed fucking valley. It was all creating some febrile cabalism in his mind. His brain was boiling like a stew pot.

As the body convulsed yet again—and much more violently this time as if it had been jolted with electricity—the mouth opened completely, the teeth parting and then coming together with a loud snapping. Whatever was going on, it was coming faster now. There were only bare seconds between each spasm now. The body heaved and shook again. The head actually lifted inches from the ground, jaws yawning wide and a perfectly audible *gaaaawwww* sort of sound came from the throat of the corpse like a ragged moan.

There was something in its mouth.

Something big.

The body jerked again and the jaws snapped open…and Spiers saw a single hairy appendage like the leg of a spider or maybe a fly emerge. It was jointed and it wiggled in the air with a fluttering motion, tapping on the lips.

Another leg joined it.

Then another.

The legs suddenly froze, as if they were aware they were being watched. But if that was the case, it didn't seem to bother them for long. Now the mouth opened as wide as it possibly could go and something forced itself out of there with a crawling, inching sort of motion…a dark leggy mass slicked with blood and clear jelly. It emerged like a swollen insect from a pupa and that was a pretty apt comparison, because what Spiers was looking at was a large, *very* large, bug. Its birth—if that's what it indeed was—had split open the VC's mouth like a pine stump struck by an axe.

Staring, his eyes feeling painted on, Spiers saw the creature was about the size of a newborn kitten. It made an unpleasant vibrating sort of sound that went right up his spine.

It hesitated there, using its many legs to clean itself.

He saw eight of them which, he remembered from 9th grade biology, made this thing an arachnid like a spider or a scorpion. But it couldn't be either of those because it was very fly-like and to add evidence to this, it extended a set of leathery wings, except they were dark and scaly like those of a bat. It fluttered them madly with a distinctive droning sound, shaking off the jelly and blood which glued them to its body.

He didn't know much about flies, but they weren't like this. They weren't this big. They didn't have spider legs and jagged bat's wings. And they sure as hell did not have a gaping oval sideways mouth filled with sharp teeth that moved from side to side or a single bulging eyeball of the sort that he found staring at him, looking so positively human and aware that he felt a weak scream building in the back of his throat.

*"What the hell is that?"* a voice said.

It was Rice. He had crawled over to see the show and if he had come to make his flesh creep, he was not disappointed.

"It came out of the VC," Spiers explained. "Right out of his mouth."

Rice just crouched there, watching it. His eyes did not blink and his face went so pale that the dirt ground into it and the camo paint streaked over it looked like streaks of black engine oil. His Adam's apple bobbed up and down.

The fly droned its wings.

It made wet, chewing sounds with its mouth.

Its eye shifted from Spiers to Rice and back again. Spiers noticed that its heavy black body was not hairy really, but covered in fine dark spines that had a metallic sheen to them. Each one was tipped in yellow, giving the creature the look of some mutant Cyclops bumblebee.

"Fuck this," Rice said, pulling his Tokarev pistol out in one smooth, fluid motion and putting three 7.62mm rounds into the thing. It oozed gouts of watery blue-black sap, spinning round and round. One of its wings was split in half and there was a gaping hole in its body that bled profusely. Its single eye took a round dead on and splashed from its housing like a burst water balloon, leaving a flaccid sort of membrane dangling from the orbit. The creature tried to fly and made it about three feet before it crashed back down again, spinning around, making a sort of whirring sound like a distant chainsaw in the woods.

What happened after that, nobody knew because there were other things going on.

The fly was no singularity.

All the mangled, bullet-ridden bodies of the Cong were shuddering, even the ones that had nearly been cut in half. And as Wick and his team of bullet-eaters and life-takers watched, flies hatched from the mouths of the dead. Dozens of them fluttered their wings and made those awful moist chewing sounds with their sideways mouths and looked around with their eyes, all of which were large with huge dark pupils.

Several of the men brought up their weapons, but Wick told them to hold fire.

They did; but it wasn't easy.

After about ten minutes maybe, the bugs had dried their wings sufficiently and lifted up into the air, rising and rising like a column of black smoke, gathering twenty feet off the ground. Then in a droning, whining mass, they took off up into the treetops and the sky beyond.

Crockett started screaming, ranting in some wounded, lunatic voice. *"...up...up...up into the sky...called by the one that spins its web in darkness..."*

Garcia went to him and tried to calm him as he thrashed on the ground, tears spilling from his eyes, saliva spilling from his mouth in glistening ropy tangles. "Inside, inside, inside," he sobbed. "Inside...*where it hurts...*"

After a time, he quieted and that was good because things were bad enough without his mania providing a soundtrack to this nightmare.

"Get your gear together," Rice said. "We're going to move."

Then, through the rising curtain of smoke and burning brush, another group trudged forward. They came with the slow yet relentless pace of the others. Some were armed, but many were not. They were all threaded with webs, not just VC in their black peasant pajamas but NVA soldiers in badly worn khaki uniforms. They came forward, the smoke of spent ordinance boiling around them, burning leaves and sticks falling on them from high above. Ghostly, dead-eyed, and cadaverous, nothing could stay their funeral march but death itself. They clomped onward with muddy boots and filth-caked feet, stepping over the remains of the others and sometimes right into them, slopping through pools of gore and viscera, bones snapping beneath their step.

It was unnerving.

"They got them bugs in 'em, too," Loony said. "Nothing but puppets. Walking puppets."

As Spiers selected yet another target, an officer with a red star on his cap, he realized that at some point fairly recently, a mixed group of hardcore NVA regulars and VC guerrillas must have come to the valley, probably to hide and lick their wounds after tangling with an American unit. Trapped, what lived here must have taken control of them somehow, erased their minds and turned them into the same sort of automatons he had seen at the POW camp. And the control factor of that was the parasitic insects they hosted. They shambled forward like living dead men.

He squeezed the trigger of the Dragunov and took out the officer with a near perfect kill shot. The officer's face splashed off his skull in a Technicolor blur of blood and flesh at the same moment his head erupted, ejecting brains and bone fragments in a vivid spray.

By then, Swede had dropped two others.

Everyone got into it then. It was another turkey shoot. The RPDs chopped the encroaching enemy into fragments, MAT-49s greasing any that made it within twenty feet of the hillside. The 56s in the hands of Garcia and Rice mopped up stragglers and the grenade launchers finished the job, frag rounds shattering the VC/NVA and white phosphorus rounds burning up what was left. A few flies vacated mouths, but not many. They died with their hosts.

Then for maybe five but no more than ten minutes (an eternity in the adrenaline-charged confines of combat), there was a welcome silence. The Marines exhaled. They blinked. Sweat and grit was rubbed from eyes. Fingers relaxed on triggers. The only sounds were more leaves and sticks falling, the crackling of burning undergrowth. The air was filled with smoke and debris, but everyone was looking at what the discharge of the grenade launchers had revealed. All around them, bodies had dropped from the trees. All of them were encapsulated in cocoons, dangling by threads of silk like party balloons, like men hanging from a scaffold. They moved with a gentle side-to-side motion.

But the worst part was that some of them were still alive.

You could see them in there, fighting and pawing at the silken shrouds. One of them finally fell. Comanche Jim and Wick went over to it, tearing that gauze free with their fingers and chopping through it with their knives, finally staring with dumb horror at the wretched, agonized figure within—an Asian man, his eyes deranged and unseeing, his mouth contorted in a wild, soundless scream. Even free of the webbing, he still clawed and writhed, hopelessly insane.

They left him there.

There was nothing they could do for him.

They joined the others in the grass.

Spiers sat there, his skin literally crawling, as he watched the still living forms in those cocoons struggling to escape.

"We can't just leave 'em like that," he said.

"One of them might be Weeks," Garcia pointed out.

The problem was that most of the silken shrouds were high above them, none less than twenty or thirty feet off the ground. Comanche Jim volunteered for tree-climbing duty, but Wick nixed the idea.

"Whatever did this is probably up there, just waiting for one of us to try something like that," he said. "No sir, those men are dead. We continue mission."

By that point, Spiers didn't give a damn about the mission, but the idea of getting out of there was a good one in his thinking.

"Look," Comanche Jim said. "Look at that."

The cocooned bodies dangling from the trees were dancing. At least, that's what it looked like. They were bouncing up and down, up and down, spinning around and around on their threads of silk. Whatever was up there was making them jump around like marionettes on a stage. It was a grisly performance. It went on for a few minutes, then stopped and the bodies just swung back and forth.

"Enough of this shit. We either get the fuck out of here or I lose my mind," Loony said, plugging a cigarette into his mouth and lighting a match off his thumbnail. He started to rise, but Gunny Rice ordered him back down.

"What?"

"Something…something else is out there," Comanche Jim said in that creepy, ominous tone that immediately got everyone's attention.

Behind them, Crockett began to make a moaning sound deep in his throat. There was something terribly prophetic about it.

Maybe not everyone felt it, but Spiers did. His nerves were jangled, his belly filled with shards of hot glass. He wanted to jump up and run, even as he wanted to hide his head and weep.

*It's coming,* he thought. *Whatever's out there is coming for us now.*

And that had no more than passed through his brain when a sound came out of the jungle, that low mournful siren-like droning he had heard in the valley when he was there with Carmody and later in the POW camp. It gained volume, sounding impossibly close, moaning through the jungle like a fog horn, hollow and deep. It rose up gradually to a high, piercing tone, then faded away. It came again, off and on, intervals of no more than five seconds in-between each blast.

"What the fuck *is* that?" Rice asked.

Wick just shook his head.

Comanche Jim kept licking his lips like there was no spit left in his mouth. Even Loony looked terrified. Crockett began to thrash on the ground, making his own wailing comment. Garcia and Spiers did what they could to calm him down.

Amoro, who rarely ever spoke, ran fingers through his Mohawk and said, "Sounds...sounds like a hunting horn."

And, yes, it did at that. The very idea stirred ancestral memories inside of Spiers. Maybe it was the tone. *The call to the hunt, the call to the hunt.* The very idea of what that implied made him feel loose and quivering inside. If it was indeed a call to the hunt, then they were without a doubt the hunted. The idea that the valley was some kind of private hunting preserve for a nameless monstrosity was the most terrifying thing he could imagine.

The call ended but it was soon replaced by something equally as threatening—that insect-like *sssskrrreeeeek!* sound that they had heard earlier right before those unseen things made to attack.

It was like a call to arms, for suddenly the jungle was alive. Not with men, but with things, *many* things. They were out there, massing and moving, turning the primeval forest into a breathing, diabolic, sentient entity. The call to the hunt had resounded through its rank, stygian depths and now the hunters had gathered in numbers—rustling, skittering, creeping through the shadows until they *were* the shadows: stalking and waiting.

They were not silent.

They saw no reason to be.

These were *their* hunting grounds; they were master here. From somewhere out there came another shrilling *ssskreek!* that had the nerve-bending tonal quality of a fork scraped over a window pane. The Marines were frozen in place, trying to choke down the involuntary screams that trembled in their throats. There was silence for maybe ten seconds, then they heard that screeching cry again, only this time it sounded almost like a question. Another screech rose above it, a loud and dominant, authoritative *SSSSSSKREEEEEK!* It was immediately answered by like cries and various trillings and pipings that seemed to come from dozens of disparate locations.

While the Marines shifted about uneasily, waiting for they knew not what, Spiers wasted no time in getting his eye to the scope of the Dragunov, scanning the jungle for silhouettes that did not belong. The perfectly insane thing was that whenever he caught sight of something, it darted away before he could get a good look at it as if it knew he was watching. It happened again and again.

Swede was studying the jungle through his scope, too, as were Wick and Rice using a spotting scope and binoculars respectively. Swede, like Spiers, kept catching quick furtive glimpses of something that did not want to be glimpsed.

Loony swore under his breath and opened up on a clump of brush with his RPD, tearing it to pieces. There was nothing there…but there had been. They all clearly saw the body of an NVA soldier dragged off into the shadows. But so quickly, no one could say what had grabbed it.

"Don't waste ammo," Rice told him. "Let the snipers do their work."

Which was perfectly logical in even the hairiest combat situation, but in the killing fields of the valley, nothing really made any sense. Everyone was teetering on the abyss of absolute chaos and no one was really sure what to do. Firing their weapons was the only thing that relieved the tension.

"Easy," Wick said, seeming to sense it. "Everyone just hold fire and wait it out. I'll tell you when to panic."

# 2

Crockett was making a whimpering sound as Garcia tried to calm him. He was nearly out of his mind by that point. Loony suggested that Garcia give him a hot shot of morphine that would put him out permanently and Comanche Jim told him to shut the fuck up.

Spiers kept watching the jungle.

*Just give me your profile for a couple seconds,* he thought. *Just a couple seconds. That's all I need to zap one of you motherfuckers.*

As he continued scanning the jungle, he let instinct guide him, shutting down everything else so there was nothing between him and his kill. He waited. He watched. He breathed in and out slowly. He kept in mind that what he was hunting was very good in the jungle, much better than any man could ever be. Whatever was out there, it knew how to camouflage itself expertly.

Then…there it was.

A shape that did not belong.

He questioned it because it was so perfectly unnatural.

What he saw in those few seconds of manic recognition was an insect-like form that was easily as large as a man if not much bigger. It was covered in a ridged, hairless cream-colored carapace with what looked like a long tail at its rear, like the stinger of a scorpion. It stood there at the edge of the jungle on a pod of segmented, chitinous legs—perhaps as many as eight—that tapered to points that looked sharp enough to thread needles. Its body was made of skeletal interlocking segments that sprouted sharp spines like those of a puffer fish, the anterior end, what would be the cephalothorax in a spider, rose up vertically like the body of a mantis, another set of jointed limbs coming out of the sides of its body at right angles like wicked mandibles.

And it had a head.

Something like a head…an oval protuberance jutting forward that was level with the mandibles. And dead center of it there was a pulsating face that sucked in and out with a yawning, slime-dripping mouth set in a vertical slit which housed a perfect ring of tusk-like teeth that gnashed independently of one another. Surrounding the slit were a dozen globular golden eyes.

And they were looking right at him, studying him the way he was studying *it* in the field of the scope. He had never seen such utter malign wrath before. The thing hated him. It wanted to exterminate him. Locking eyes with that horror made something inside him close up like an orchid.

The entire episode probably lasted five seconds, if that. Then the creature disappeared in a flurry of legs.

He never even squeezed the trigger.

*No, and you didn't because you were terrified of the idea that if you didn't kill it, it would come for you. And when it seized you in those killing mandibles and put its grotesque crawling face inches from your own, you would go stark screaming mad…*

Maybe the others began to see the creatures, too, because they started shooting. They didn't give a damn what Major Wick shouted at them or that Gunny Rice threatened to personally core their asses, they needed to shoot. Fuck professionalism and fuck the elite standards of Force Recon, they sensed the threat out there pressing in and they were going to do something about it. So they all opened up, knocking down trees and ripping apart the vegetation and punching holes into the jungle.

Finally, Wick got them under control.

They had probably cooked off an easy hundred rounds combined and had not a hit a thing. At least, anything that they could see.

Amoro fed a new drum magazine into his RPD. His silence and unreadable face gave no indication of what he was thinking or feeling. Regardless of the situation, he always looked the same. Suddenly, he stood up. Rice told him to get down, but he ignored him. He'd had his fill and it was obvious. He let out a wild and whopping rebel yell and ran down the hillside, firing the light machinegun, putting out bursts in every direction. Since what was out there wouldn't bring the fight to him, he was bringing it to them.

"GET SOME!" he cried out as he dodged about, shooting and shooting, ejected brass casings spinning through the air. "COME AND GET SOME! *GET SOME! GET SOME!"*

Loony cheered as Rice swore and Wick pounded his fists uselessly against the ground.

Amoro made it about twenty-five feet before he stopped as if he had hit a wall and the RPD slid from his hands and thudded into the grass. Something had hit him in the throat and that was apparent to everyone on the hilltop. They thought it was a crossbow bolt. It went in right through his voice box and exploded out the back of his neck with a plug of meat. It was lodged there. With all the blood, no one could say what it was.

But Spiers saw.

Through his scope, he saw that what was in Amoro's neck— like a black horn—was connected to a fine thread of web that trailed off into the jungle. Amoro gasped and the line was jerked taut and he literally flew off his feet, pulled off into the brush with incredible force and speed, tearing through the bushes and bouncing off tree trunks.

That was it.

He was gone.

And it happened faster than anyone could possibly react.

No one said anything.

Not for a moment or two.

Then, amazingly, it was Garcia who broke the silence. "Fuck this shit," he said, charging down the hillside with his Type 56 assault rifle until he reached the spot where Amoro had gotten hit. Down on his belly in the blood-spattered grass, he took up the RPD and began putting out a volume of fire into the jungle. And that did it. Comanche Jim and Loony and Swede charged out there, shooting and ducking until they reached Garcia. Wick and Rice had no choice but to follow suit. Spiers was right behind them, towing Crockett who stumbled about like a child just learning to walk.

When everyone was spread out in a skirmish line, Gunny Rice vented. "YOU IDIOT! YOU USELESS DUMBFUCK SUICIDAL INBRED HALF-WIT MOTHERFUCKER!" he shouted at Garcia. "YOU'VE JUST PUT ALL OUR LIVES ON THE LINE WITH

YOUR FUCKING JOHN WAYNE COWBOY BULLSHIT! WE GET BACK, YOU'RE OUT OF RECON! YOU'LL BE CLEANING FUCKING TOILETS AND POLISHING BOOTS AND SCRUBBING CUM STAINS OUT OF MY FUCKING SHORTS! YOU'LL BE SO THOROUGHLY BENT OVER AND GANG-FUCKED BY THE CORPS THAT YOU WON'T TOUCH PUSSY FOR SIX MONTHS!"

He would have went on, but Wick told him to pipe down. There was no doubt that what Garcia had done was stupid—drawing them all out into the open so they could die an ugly death like Amoro. But now they were here and they had to make the best of it. That was how Recon worked. No matter what kind of shit you got drawn into, you adjusted to it and adapted and turned a zero into a plus.

Comanche Jim was watching the jungle very carefully. "We're like meat waiting for the worms," was how he appraised the situation.

"Affirmative on that," Rice said.

Everyone was waiting for what Wick would come up with. He was pissed off at Amoro for dying on him and Garcia for putting them all at a worse risk than they already were. But he would work with it. He had more experience than any of them. This was his third tour with Recon.

"Okay, Garcia," he said. "You got hero's blood in you today. So take that RPD and lead us into the jungle. Anything moves, you grease it. Hump it!"

The fighting gleam had gone out of Garcia's eyes, but he knew better than to refuse a direct order.

Comanche Jim, who had been studying every shadow and every clump of brush, shook his head. "Sir, you can't let him—"

"I want your fucking opinion I'll ask for it," Wick snapped at him.

Spiers knew what was happening here. The jungle was filled with those things and Comanche Jim knew that Wick was sending Garcia right into their numbers. He was sending him to his death. That's how Garcia was going to make up for his lack of protocol, his break in unit discipline. This, in Wick's thinking, was how a Marine, a good Marine, squared things up and paid his dues. For a combat soldier, this was the ultimate act of contrition and compensation.

Garcia steeled himself, then he moved off towards the jungle in a zigzag, expecting death. He made it maybe twenty feet, then he paused and watched the jungle. Then he moved again. When he was near the treeline there was a quick, shrill *ssskreek!* and everyone knew it was about to happen but there wasn't a damn thing they could do about it because there were no targets, there was nothing to fight against, nothing to throw any covering fire at.

Or maybe there was.

Garcia came up out of his crouch and fired a few bursts from his RPD and then a strand of web shot out of the trees and knocked his boonie hat from his head. He had about enough time to gasp before a second strand came down from overhead and this one drilled right through his shoulder and anchored itself to the ground. He cried out and everyone saw the droplets of blood running down the strand. He fought against it, pulled against it, but its tensile strength was unbelievable. Another strand shot through his throat and then two more impaled him in the torso. Like the first, they went right through him, anchoring themselves to the ground. Within seconds, a half dozen more strands skewered him. And by then, he had dropped the RPD, shrieking in agony, the strands or fibers glistening with his blood. Other than that, they were barely even visible. The sunlight shined on them like monofilament fishing line.

"Can't we—" Spiers started to say, just sick about it.

"No," Wick told him. "On my signal, we move."

There had to have been no less than thirty or forty of those web strands piercing Garcia by then. He was lifted up from the ground, dangling and kicking like some kind of puppet, doing a morbid jig that gradually slowed as the blood drained out of him. By the time he lost consciousness, he was no longer moving. There wasn't so much as a reflexive twitch left in him. Then he began to rise higher and higher as what lurked in the trees above began to draw him up to his grisly destiny. The strands were not pulled up; no, they remained firmly anchored to the ground.

It was Garcia alone that was rising.

He slid up the strands with a sound like a bootlace being drawn tightly through an eyelet. It was an awful sound and Spiers clutched his hands to his ears so he did not have to hear it. Seconds later, Garcia disappeared into the canopy overhead. By then, the jungle had gone quiet. Whatever had been out there was gone.

"Let's get the fuck out of here," Wick said.

# 𝕫

They pushed on for another hour, hacking forward through bamboo and ferns and knotted tendrils of jungle and then they came into a clearing. A huge clearing. They walked out into it, beaten, empty, horrified.

It looked like a field of scarecrows.

But they weren't scarecrows.

Spread before them were the bodies of literally hundreds of men, women, and children wired to stakes or impaled upon them. A forest of deadwood limbs and leeched sunless faces and screaming skulls. Many were so very ancient they were dressed in mildewed rags, their bones splintered and pitted. They were coming apart like mummies fashioned out of straw. Still others were fresh, flesh intact, but were drained into prune-like, wrinkled things. American soldiers, Viet Cong, NVA. Peasants. All strewn with webs like dead flies on a windowsill. So many and in such variety nobody could seem to take it all in. They wandered amongst the shattered husks and cadavers and skeletons with an almost religious awe.

Spiers was with them, turning from one fright to the next, stumbling through that cornfield of human, bloodless stalks enshrouded with webbing.

By the time they broke back into the forest on the other side, they were pale, faces drawn, teeth chattering, eyes bulging from their heads. They moved through the cocooned forest decorated with its lacework of webs and suddenly one of them—Rice— screamed and disappeared.

Spiers saw it happen.

Rice stepped forward and the ground swallowed him up. They went to where he had been and there was a hole leading down into the earth. A black and putrescent effluvium wafted up out of there. Wick dropped a rock down there and no one heard it hit bottom.

"Whole area must be honeycombed," Comanche Jim said. "Better watch where you step...trapdoors everywhere...we're right on top of the lair."

The jungle started to peter out, but still the trees were high and blighted and slick with sinister shadows. Swede cried out as a gob of webs struck him in the face, enveloping his head. It was connected from above by a long, trailing vine-like rope of the stuff. Before it was drawn taut and he was yanked up into the greenery above, Comanche Jim leaped, his machete in hand. He swung at the cord of web and it vibrated with a shrill pinging sort of sound. Then he brought the machete down again with everything he had and the cord was severed. Swede hit the ground thrashing and squealing.

Spiers and Wick took hold of him and peeled the webs free. They writhed in their hands, each individual strand alive like the tentacle of a squid. The mass pulled free of Swede's face with a perfectly awful sound like roots yanked from the earth and the reason for that was easy to see: in those scant seconds the mass had been glued to his face, it had sent out tiny filaments that penetrated into his cheeks and lips. When the mass was gone, he crawled away, a dozen tiny pinholes in his skin, each one dripping blood. Nearly out of his mind, he pawed at them, smearing his face with red war paint.

Up above, they could hear wet, slopping sounds like something beyond imagining was licking its lips.

That was it.

Control was lost.

Everyone started yelling and shooting and shell casings were flying and branches and leaves were dropping...and then something big came spinning end over end from above. It struck Comanche Jim and knocked him flat. He let out a high, wailing sound and kicked it free of him.

It was a mummified body, shrunken and drained, eyes sucked into its skull. There was no doubt that it was Garcia.

Wick, seeing something they didn't, made a grab for the body. It was dragged away through the brush, then up into the trees, still connected by a length of silk.

"One by one by one," Loony said. "That how it's gonna work. By the time we get where we're going, ain't gonna be none of us left."

Even Wick didn't have the heart by that point to tell him he was wrong or dress him down for jabbering in an unprofessional manner. Because he was right. He was absolutely right and they knew it. They had come to kill the thing or *things* that hunted the valley and it was they who were being killed. They had inflicted but a scratch thus far to their unseen, inhuman enemy. They were being played and tormented. The way things were going, none of them would ever even find what they were fighting and have a good crack at killing it.

"We could call for extraction," Spiers said. And even when that met with stony stares, he still tried to rationalize it. "There were ten of us when we started this pig fuck and now there's six left. Crockett needs medical attention. He's fucked up and you know it and it's not just psychological either. There's something physically wrong with him. Jesus, just look at him."

They did and there was no doubt he was in a bad way. He could barely keep on his feet. His eyes were glazed and there was an awful tic in the corner of his mouth. Cords jumped in his throat and his entire body trembled. He did not even moan any more. He was done in.

"We continue mission," Wick said.

*The fucking asshole,* Spiers thought. He was dangerously obsessed. Spiers had heard that these special operations types were smart. That they fought unconventionally, following no set patterns, striking where no one could strike and fading into the night, daring to do the most impossible things and often achieving them by sheer guts, bravado, stealth, and creative thinking. And here was Wick, kicking all that into the gutter, a typical brain-dead jarhead push-button Marine without the common sense to wipe his own ass with.

"With all due respect, *sir,*" Spiers said. "All you're going to accomplish here is getting us killed. You're fighting something that's beyond you. Something we can't handle."

"Bullshit," Wick said.

"No bullshit about it, sir. None whatsoever. We've been played ever since we came into this valley. You think you're leading us to a target, but you're not. You're being *led.* Those things are watching us right now and they know where we're going and they know what it is we think we're going to do."

"And we'll do it," Wick said. "Because that's our job."

Loony laughed. "Damn right. If a chopper came right now, I wouldn't get on it. You know why? Because I'm Recon and I don't stop. They probably don't teach you fucking snipers that. You pussies hide behind trees and pop the enemy from half a mile away. Not us. That's not how we operate. We like it close in and personal. And if you don't like that, start walking. You might reach base in a couple weeks."

Spiers looked over at Swede who looked away and then at Comanche Jim because he thought he might be the only one with common sense, but Comanche Jim was ignoring him. He was like the others. They were fixed on this objective and they would see it through. Nothing else mattered except mission completion. Nothing. And maybe it was more than being brainwashed robots, maybe it was a matter of personal honor and unit integrity. These guys were Marine Force Recon. Nobody had ever fucked them up like those things in the jungle and that was an insult that could not go unanswered.

So be it.

"All right," Spiers said. "Let's go. The trap is just ahead."

They started walking. They weren't even bothering with the usual patrol formation. No point man. No tail. Nothing. They marched in single file with Wick out front and Comanche Jim in the back, Spiers stuck there trying to drag Crockett along because if he didn't, those gung ho bushmasters would have left him behind to rot.

The farther they got into the rotting green latticework of the jungle, the worse the going got. Everything was damp, slippery, and treacherous. Fallen trees and rotting stumps were furry with greasy moss. Ferns and fan leaves felt unpleasantly warm and oily as they brushed against bare arms or the backs of hands. This was thick vine forest that had to be hacked through. Everything was wet and crawling and dank. Spiers fought his way forward, trying to tow Crockett as his boots sank three inches into the slopping black mud with every step.

Crockett, of course, was oblivious to it all.

He mumbled now and again, but Spiers had no idea what he was saying. His eyes were red and swollen, his breathing shallow and rattling. Every step was hard work. A rank feverish heat came off him in sickening waves. He wouldn't make it much farther, but Spiers planned on pulling him along until one of them dropped from exhaustion. Which, realistically, couldn't be too far in the future. The land around them was dotted by one green, shaggy hill after another. Spiers' calves were aching, his shoulder sore from supporting Crockett, and sweat was gushing out of him despite the salt tablets he'd swallowed.

The only positive thing was that there was no immediate threat in the jungle. Birds were screeching in the trees, monkeys whooping, and lizards croaking. A good indication that there were no predators on the hunt.

*Maybe we'll get there,* he thought. *Maybe we'll really reach the target, but we won't be in any shape to fight by then.*

He seemed to get a masochistic delight out of the idea.

Thirty minutes later on the slope of a rugged hillside, Crockett's legs went and he folded right up. Try as he might, Spiers couldn't get him back up. He was done in. Unconscious. There was no way to rouse him. Not without Garcia's medical bag and the ammonia stick in it. Crockett was dead weight.

"Well?" Wick asked.

"I don't know," Spiers said, seeing the lethal gleam in his eye and trying to figure out some way of buying Crockett some time. "He's in a bad way and we've been pushing him too hard."

Loony giggled at that as if it was the most preposterous thing he'd ever heard. Comanche Jim looked down at Crockett impassively as did Swede. They were all killers and Spiers knew it. If Wick gave the word, they'd slit Crockett's throat. They would do anything to preserve mission integrity. Especially now after the hardships and heartbreaks of this op. There was a blood vengeance in their eyes; they needed to repay what had reduced them to this sorry state. Nothing else mattered.

Wick studied the forested hillsides around them. He consulted his compass and then his map. "All right. We're wasting daylight here. We should have been at the target two hours ago. I don't like that. I don't accept failure of any sort," he said, staring at Spiers. "We have three choices. We leave Crockett and swing back for him later…if such a thing is possible. We waste him right now. Or you stay behind with him and, again, hopefully we'll rendezvous with you later. But there's no guarantee of that."

"I'll stay with him."

"Don't be a dumbass, Spear-chucker. We got the radio, you don't," Loony said. "You think you can find your way out of here alone? Animals'll be picking your fucking bones in a week."

But Spiers didn't give a shit.

He was drawing his line in the sand right here.

"I don't know what fucking Marine Corps you people are with, but the one I'm in says a Marine does not leave another Marine behind. I'll stay. Go on your merry way. I hope those fucking things get you all. It's what you deserve."

Loony giggled again. "Awwwww, poor little Spear-chucker. Have we offended your little sense of esprit de corps? Did we ruin your comic book fucking preconceptions about special ops and loyalty and brothers in arms? Did we piss all over your flag-waving jack-off fantasies about what this war is really about?"

"That'll do," Wick said.

Spiers didn't get mad.

What was the point?

There was nothing like war to destroy all your fantasies and preconceptions. He held no high ideals about any unit in that war. When he had joined the Marines, there were bugles playing in his head and he had rigid standards concerning glory and patriotism. Eight months of bloody, ugly, desensitizing combat had straightened him out. Glory and patriotism were for mothers who had to justify burying their nineteen-year-old sons in windy graveyards. Glory and patriotism were for politicians who had to manipulate, brainwash, and inflame the public into supporting a war in which they would have to make the ultimate sacrifice of their children. Glory and patriotism were for the home front where you could espouse high ideals and you didn't have to look at the human wreckage of conflict: dead children, burning babies, screaming villagers, and young men with their guts hanging out. In combat, there was only survival. There was nothing more. There was no flag-waving or trumpets or the rousing drum rolls, there was only staying alive. And nobody knew that better than Spiers. There were no bugles in his head anymore, only the funereal scratching of minor-key violins droning through his skull.

"It's all right, Major. He doesn't bother me," Spiers said. "'Nam has made me real slippery. Nothing sticks to me anymore."

"I'll stay with 'em," Swede said.

"Hell you will," Wick told him. "We need you. Spiers wants to nursemaid, let him. *We* have a mission and *we* will see it through."

Nobody argued with him, not even Spiers...though he almost did start laughing, wanting to ask Major Dumbass which John Wayne movie he was quoting from.

Comanche Jim helped him turn Crockett over. They stripped his weapons and web belt free so he could be more comfortable. They slid his arms through the straps of his rucksack, but it wouldn't come off.

"It's stuck to him," Spiers said.

Comanche Jim started pulling on it and Spiers was going to tell him to take it easy, not to hurt Crockett. But Crockett was beyond pain. His red-lidded eyes fluttered and drool spilled from his mouth but that was about it. While Loony kept an eye out for trouble with his RPD, Wick got into the act, too, as did Swede. The pack was stuck and there had to be a reason for it. Spiers held onto Crockett while the others tried to work the pack free. It was oddly stuck to his back, the center of his back. Crockett's breath was fetid, sour-smelling yet oddly sweet and sickening like a decomposing corpse. He barely breathed. In Spiers' arms, he was shrunken, a bag of bones and very little else.

"Hell is going on here?" Wick said as they struggled with the pack.

All together, they gave it one last good pull and it came away with a sticky sound. A violent seizure passed through Crockett's body and he went limp in Spiers arms. And from inside the pack, there was a muted shrill squealing noise.

Wick dropped the pack. "Jesus," he said.

There were dozens of tiny white fibers connecting the pack to Crockett's back. They threaded out of it and into him. Many of them were pink with blood. Not stained with it, but pink because they were hollow inside and *filled* with blood. Comanche Jim pulled out his big Marine Bowie knife and began sawing through them on by one. As he did so, his face screwed up into a mask of rage and revulsion, blood ran from the severed threads and whatever they were connected to—inside the pack—made that squealing sound again.

Wick kicked the pack and then kicked it again.

Then he emptied it out. Gear fell free and so did something else. At first sight, Spiers thought it was a small, wriggling brain because that's what it looked like. It was a swollen, greasy thing about the size of a ripe grapefruit, fissured down the center like a human brain, its surface steel-gray and convoluted. It was one of the spiders that Crockett had picked up in the web he'd been trapped in. But it wasn't a spider, of course, but something more along the lines of a blood-sucking tick. It was so swollen with blood that it had to drag itself along with vestigial-looking legs, a bloated and pulsating fleshy mass trailing web strands.

Wick pulled out his Russian Tokarev pistol and put a bullet into it. It screamed with the high whining voice of a child and exploded with a gushing spray of meaty ichor, a grayish slime that oozed and bubbled in the grass. Its flaccid body looked like some deflated grisly party balloon, legs still bicycling.

Spiers, bile rising up the back of his throat, pushed Crockett away from him, running his hands over himself, searching for stray ticks. *He was pressed up against you for hours,* a mocking voice in his head informed him. *Anything might have passed from him to you.* He wasn't satisfied until he checked every inch of his body and emptied out his pack and ammo bag, looked in every pocket.

When Spiers got himself put back together, Loony—who found it all morbidly hilarious—licked his dry lips and said, "If you feel something crawling along your spine, Spear-chucker, just tell yourself it's only an itch, it's only an itch."

Comanche Jim checked Crockett for a pulse, but there was nothing. "He's dead. Fucking thing was draining him."

There was no time to bury him and no one liked the idea of touching him, so they moved out to their final destination. It took some time before Spiers no longer felt tiny leggy things crawling up his back or up between his legs.

# 13

An hour later, they found what they were looking for.

There was no mistaking it.

It broke free from the hilly green jungle in an immense rising mound that must have been several hundred feet in circumference, the apex of which was thirty if not forty feet above them. It was covered with a snaking accretion of vines and creepers, rocky ledges and bushy vegetation. This was the lair of the creatures.

"This is it," Wick said. "Let's do this."

"Do what?" Spiers asked him. "What is it we're supposed to do?"

"Kill monsters, sunshine," Loony said.

*Really? Is that what this is really about?* Spiers wondered because he didn't really believe it for a moment. The mound— what he could see of it—was too symmetrical to be of natural origin. There was something exceedingly strange about it. It was more than what he saw, but what he *felt.* Something about it…so primeval, so unnatural…made the hairs stand up on the back of his neck. He was filled with a gnawing sense of anxiety and horror. It sprouted black wings and flew through him. He felt completely impotent and helpless staring up at it. There was something ominous and dreadful about it and he was seized by the unreasoning need to scream.

The lair.

*The lair.*

*The lair.*

The words echoed around in his skull until it felt as if he was unraveling inside. He stood there, awe-struck, mindless, irrational in his terror.

"C'mon, Spiers," Wick told him. "Time to put this nightmare to rest. Do it for Gunny Carmody. You owe him that."

And yes, yes, he certainly did.

He did at that.

Yet…now that he was here, he wanted to throw his weapons and run off into the jungle and bury himself in their steaming rank depths. The need to do so was nearly overwhelming.

*YOU GET YOUR PRETTY PINK FRILLY FAIRY ASS IN GEAR, CHERRY, AND HUMP THAT RUCK AND GET THAT WEAPON IN YOUR HANDS!* he could hear Carmody shouting at him. *YOU QUIT THAT GIRL SCOUT POO NANNY WHINING AND DRY UP THE PISS BETWEEN YOUR LEGS! WHO DO YOU THINK YOU ARE, YOU GODDAMN NUT-GRABBING FAGGOT? MISS MARY JANE SWEET SLIT WAITING FOR A HAND TO HOLD AND A COCK TO PULL? YOU ARE A FUCKING U.S. MARINE! YOU ARE A FUCKING KILLER! SO PULL UP YOUR SKIRT AND PLUCK YOUR TEE TEE PECKER OUT FROM BETWEEN YOUR SHAVED LEGS AND GET THAT MOTHERFUCKER SWINGING FROM SIDE TO SIDE LIKE A REAL MAN! GET SOME STEEL IN YOUR BALLS AND SOME IRON IN YOUR PANTS AND SHOOT YOUR LOAD DOWN THE ENEMY'S THROAT! DON'T YOU DARE MAKE A MOCKERY OF ME AND WHAT I TAUGHT YOU! DON'T YOU THINK FOR ONE HAIRY BALL-SUCKING MOMENT THAT YOU WILL DISGRACE ME OR MY BELOVED MARINE CORPS! HOP TO IT OR I SWEAR TO CHRIST I WILL COME BACK AND PERSONALLY SODMIZE YOUR SHITHOLE WITH MY CLENCHED FIST!!!*

The voice was so real, so incredibly authentic, that he felt a tear slide from his eye.

"Goddammit, move!" Wick snapped at him and it was no casual request.

Spiers started climbing.

The mound looked, if anything, like the spout of an anthill, the base of it littered with gray bones, ragged flaps of clothing, and jawless skulls green with mold tangled in the roots of creepers. Wick led them up with Comanche Jim close behind, then Swede, Spiers next in line with Loony. They moved quickly but carefully, searching for handholds and footholds amongst the knotted hairy vines and blooming vibrant orchids. Up, up, they went, higher and higher, rocks and sticks rolling down through the brush below them. The jungle to all sides was silent and eerie. Whatever this place truly was, no animals came within a half a mile of it. They felt the odious vibes and it scared them away. The atmosphere was beyond bad, it was fucking toxic, it was deadly.

*This is it,* Spiers thought as they moved precariously upwards. *This is it. You either pull this off or it ends right here.*

At the very moment this went through his mind, Swede stepped down and sank right into the earth up to his knee. He pulled himself free easily enough, but as he did so there was a sudden droning sound and winged creatures began flying up out of the hole he had made with his boot. Flies. Those same mutant flies that had crawled from the mouths of the dead VC. Dozens of them came up out of the hole as if he had stepped into a hive. One of them flew right into his face and, before he could ward it off, it attached itself with the sharp tips of its eight legs, which looked very much like chitinous, hooked nails. Spiers clearly saw its needle-like teeth bite into Swede's eye like a plump grape.

He screamed.

He thrashed.

He went down to one knee.

By then, there were three or four of them on him. He dropped his weapon and seized one of them in his hands, rending it apart. It made a sharp whirring sound as he did so, bubbling black goo squirting down his arms. Within scant seconds, he was covered in flies. They were tearing into him with their savage little side-to-side mouths, ripping open his flesh with the gnawing sounds of many interlocking teeth. By then, Swede had disappeared. He was an animate, screaming mass of flies, blood bursting in the air, squirting out between the swollen bodies of his tormentors.

Spiers and Loony tried to get to him, but he fell, rolling down the hillside, squishing the flies beneath him. By the time he made it to the bottom, he was no longer screaming. He was a twisted, shuddering mass of blood and tissue and broken fly anatomy. The heads of the flies hung on by their teeth, even divorced of their bodies the jaws kept biting and biting.

It all happened incredibly fast.

Swede was dead.

Those flies that survived the barrel roll to the bottom, took wing and flew away.

"Let's go," Wick said, disinterested in anything now but what waited above.

Spiers, his head held low, followed the others up.

At the apex, the mound flattened out like the top of a beer can, fifty or sixty feet across and like a beer can it had an opening—a spout cut right into the earth. It was so big around, you could've dropped a bulldozer through the mouth.

"Okay," Wick said, his gray-streaked buzzcut almost completely white now. "We came to do some killing, so let's do it already."

But Spiers wasn't moving as Comanche Jim and Wick climbed into their harnesses, joining their ropes together and tying them off to a stout root. They seemed so matter-of-fact about the whole thing it was crazier than just about anything thus far.

"C'mon, Spiers, hop to," Wick said, clipping a flashlight to his web belt.

But Spiers wasn't hopping to. He was staring down the throat of that tunnel and smelling that awful, rotting stink and waiting for a spider the size of a Mack truck to come running up at them.

"You gotta be kidding me," he finally said. "Down there? Fuck that, we found its hole, now let's call in an airstrike and burn that sonofabitch out or bury it alive."

Wick seemed unconcerned. He tossed the coil of rope down into the darkness and hooked his harness to it. "You can stay up here if you want. It's up to you. You can keep Loony company."

Loony grinned.

"Goddammit!" Spiers said, totally frustrated and worn wire-thin by that point. "Why in the fuck did you drag me on this goddamn safari? Why the hell did you need me?"

Comanche Jim disappeared down the shaft. Wick followed suit.

"Because," he called up at him, "we needed you to verify our position. Had to know we were in the right place…"

And then his voice trailed off, echoing away into subterranean depths.

And Spiers was alone, pretty sure he was completely insane. He stood there. Waited. Worried. Paced. Smoked one cigarette after the other and prayed for capture by some hardcore—but normal—

NVA unit and knew he might as well have prayed for naked women to parachute from the sky.

Just wasn't gonna happen.

He hated the VC and NVA like everyone in that war, but he had to give them credit. At least they weren't stupid enough to frequent this valley. And when they lost people here, they let it lie and got the hell out.

He turned to Loony. "What's so fucking important about this?"

"How should I know, Spear-chucker? I just follow orders."

Which was bullshit, of course.

He knew something, only he wasn't going to tell. That was part of the game these guys played. Spiers knew damn well that after they were briefed on an op—particularly a highly classified op—Force Recon teams went into enforced isolation so that there was no possibility of any intelligence leaks. He wasn't at that briefing so he didn't go in with them. But Loony had been there. He probably didn't know as much as Wick did, but he had to know something.

"Why don't you just tell me what this is about?" Spiers finally said, lighting a cigarette. "Can't hurt now. Who am I going to tell?"

"No one. And that's how we're keeping things."

"C'mon, Loony."

"Fuck you. You want to know something, you ask Major Wick."

"I tried that."

"And?"

"He said I didn't have an Omega clearance. What the hell is an Omega clearance?"

"If you don't know what it is, then I can't tell you. Just keep your nose clean, Spear-chucker. Don't stick it where it don't belong."

"Shit."

Spiers watched the sun drifting towards the horizon. It would be dark in a couple hours. He wondered if they'd still be alive by then. A month from now they'd probably all be KIA-BNR. He smoked in silence for a time, then he said, "What if Wick and Swede and Comanche Jim don't come back? What then?"

"Then we go down."

"Not me."

"Guess again. I'm going and you're going with me."

"Why? I don't even know what I'm looking for."

"I'll tell you when the time comes."

"Tell me now."

"Shut the fuck up."

So that's where it stood for the next few minutes. Spiers watched the opening and Loony seemed to watch everything else. He moved along the perimeter of the mound, keeping an eye on the encroaching jungle below. Every time a stick cracked or a stone broke loose from its own weight and rolled down, he checked it out, always listening, always watching.

A rustling came from the far side and he went over there. "Nothing," he said. "It's always nothing."

"One of these times it might be something," Spiers told him.

"Sure."

Guy wasn't much for conversation.

Loony swore under his breath and then made a coughing sound.

Spiers had his back to him, pulling off another cigarette, watching the hole. "You know," he said, "we're in this shit together so you might as well tell me. It'll give us something to talk about."

Silence.

"Loony?"

*Shit.*

He turned around and Loony was gone. He was alone on top of the mound. He ran around the perimeter, shouting, "LOONY! LOONY! *LOOOOOONEEEEE! WHERE THE FUCK ARE YOU?"*

But there was no reply, only the sound of his voice echoing out amongst the green hills and black misty hollows between them. Something had taken Loony and taken him silently. There wasn't a sign of anything.

Jesus.

Down in the jungle there were sounds…secretive rustlings and slitherings.

Spiers stood there for another moment or two, listening to the eerie sounds all around him and staring down at all those bones. He crushed his cigarette beneath his boot and climbed into his harness.

And went down.

24

It was like the nest of a spider.

Just a seething, sticky mass of webs strung with the bodies of the dead and drained, shot through with dozens and dozens of funneled passages. Spiers had a flashlight, MAT-49, sidearm, machete, three grenades…but no way to mark his progress through the nest, no way to be sure he would ever come out again. Just no way.

He crawled on his hands and knees through intersecting passages, hearing sounds, but never sure if he made them or something else did. He wanted to be scared, *should've* been scared, but somehow, he wasn't. Numb, maybe. Empty, maybe. But not exactly frightened by that point. He'd been through too goddamn much. Somehow, it all seemed inevitable. It was Fate and you couldn't fight Fate.

*This is where it's been leading me,* he thought. *My whole life has been leading me right here.*

There was no peace or vindication in that, only acceptance. Mindless, blank-eyed acceptance of his own impending destruction.

His light bobbed and he waited for something—he didn't know what exactly—to come charging through the tunnels at him. But it didn't happen. That webby material seemed pretty solid, but at any time, he supposed, it could tear and pitch him into some black subterranean hell far below.

He thought: *This is for Carmody. Just keep that in mind. If you win, if you kill what's waiting in this place, then it's for you. But not now. Not yet…*

Now and again he could hear weird echoing sounds, big sounds as if something very large was moving, rustling, shifting. But others, too, small sounds like snatches of human voices coming from some distant, secret location.

He pressed on.

He was bathed with sweat and that gauzy web-stuff felt like sticky fiberglass insulation. It made his palms itch. A nightmare, a goddamn nightmare. He had to find Comanche Jim and Wick. They had the rocket launchers. There was safety for the man that held those tubes—nothing could hope to stand against them.

At least, he hoped nothing could.

He kept going and then the passage widened, opened up until it was like a cavern before him, some dire vacuum of horror. A cavern set with an impenetrable darkness. That hot, black stink of decay was so thick you could've filled a cup with it.

Carefully then, submachine gun and flashlight held out before him, Spiers crept forward, sounds echoing around him, shadows crawling, a strange and pestilent breeze blowing into his face. He could see that the passage ended just ahead, the floor falling away into some oddly funnel-shaped depression.

A light exploded in his face. "You made it, eh?" Wick said, his face beaded with drops of perspiration. He held a finger to his lips. "Be quiet…I think it's down that hole."

Spiers tried to quiet his hammering heart. He wiped sweat from his face. It was warm and humid in there. His fatigues felt like they were wringing wet.

"Somebody want to tell me what this is about?" he asked.

Comanche Jim, who waited a few feet away, said, *"Quiet."*

Wick played his light over the opening of the funnel and Spiers could see that it had to be an easy fifty or sixty feet across, the mouth of some infernal channel that led into the blackest depths of the earth.

A sort of distant droning rose up like a locust in a summer field…and then faded.

"Shit," Spiers heard himself say.

The three of them waited, fingers trembling on triggers, hearts pounding, breath wheezing in lungs.

Below, echoing up at them, they could hear wet sounds like something big moving through a swamp. Those sounds were enough to inspire a dozen forms of cold, crawling madness. Their minds were picturing things, immense spider-like forms that lived in that dank, dripping blackness.

The sounds started to get closer, closer. An echoing, thrumming noise like hissing and breathing and it seemed to be almost on top of them, almost close enough to touch…and then it stopped.

They sat there in that sunless, godless womb, shivering and sweating and forcing their stomachs to stay down because that acrid stink filled the air. It was like turpentine and formaldehyde, things pickled and salted by acidic chemicals. It was one of the creatures. There was no doubt of that; nothing else could smell that unnatural. The fumes coming off it made them giddy.

"I'll take a look again," Wick whispered.

Spiers could hear him crawling through the sticky material, hear his equipment bumping and thudding and snagging and it seemed to take him a long time, even though the mouth of the chasm was no more than fifteen, twenty feet away. But time had gone rubbery, elastic. Like most natural forces, it seemed to have no place here.

Wick clicked on his light.

Comanche Jim let out a muted cry.

Wick never had time to do anything.

The creature was waiting for him.

It was sitting there, clinging to the lip of the chasm like some great and impossible insect about the size of a pickup truck…or maybe two of them. It was the same sort of thing Spiers had seen through the scope, only much, much larger. Its body was wide and low, cream-colored, roughly figure eight-shaped, like two plated discs joined together, each of which seemed to be formed of interlocking segments. Not smooth in the least, but chitinous and ridged, convoluted with bony furrows and narrow staves like ribs, lots of knobs and hollows set between. And spines. A series of them rose from its dorsal plates and each of them looked long enough to skewer a man. Obscenely skeletal, the creature had at least ten legs, maybe as many as a dozen, each big around as a fence post and jointed like those of a crab. A sheer membrane of flesh webbed them together at the upper extremities. At each leg was a bulging pod that oozed nets of spreading, living webs.

It looked like a living exoskeleton

There were easily a dozen of the grotesque bat-winged flies on it. They seemed to be picking away at something, perhaps feeding off the creature's parasites.

"Easy," Comanche Jim said in a low voice.

Wick just waited there, mere feet from the thing and easily within striking distance.

Spiers thought it was some kind of spider because that's how it looked…or almost. But it was no spider. No goddamn spider ever born had a tail and this thing had a tail. From its ass-end…or what he thought was its ass-end…there was a tail that was thick as a telephone pole and easily thirty feet long. It was segmented and pale, looking like a spinal column or maybe the body of some huge nightmare tapeworm. It curled up and above the creature, trembling, wanting to be put to use. There were two ghastly white hooks at the end of it like pincers.

Wick was frozen, trying to think of what to do.

Comanche Jim had the beast in his sights, but he hesitated in shooting. If he didn't kill it outright, it would kill Wick. There was no question of that.

Spiers just watched it.

Like the one he'd spied through the scope, this one had the same body plan with its forward section held vertical and erect like a praying mantis. That part of it rose up to about twelve feet and was protected by a segmented carapace. Its two upper hook-like mandibles were held high in a threat posture. And there was its forward protruding head with that grotesque pulsing face, the vertical slit opening to reveal the ring of gnashing teeth and the surrounding circle of golden eyes which were beady and glistening. They seemed to be watching Wick. The head cocked to the side and the mouth opened. It made a high-pitched *sssskrrreeeeek!* sound that almost sounded like a question, as if it was trying to communicate with him. *Sssskrrreeeeek? Sssskrrreeeeek?*

But the nuance of that was lost on Wick; he was struck dumb by its presence.

It let out another *sssskrrreeeeek!* followed by a series of trilling noises and something like the purring of a kitten.

A very unfunny voice in the back of Spiers' mind said, *take me to your leader.*

And the creature looked at him.

The fan of its teeth parted and copious amounts of sharp-smelling saliva oozed out. From the acidic stink, he thought it might be some sort of digestive juice.

It looked at him with flat, black hatred.

Its jointed mandibles shivered, making chitinous clicking sounds as they extended, then withdrew.

It raised a leg slowly, then another…as if in indecision. Spiers had the oddest feeling that it didn't know what to do, that it was not at all used to its prey invading its lair.

Its entire body was shuddering now, pissing out a pungent steam of noxious vapor that burned his nostrils. But the very worst thing, is that he could hear it breathing. Sucking in air with a hollow sound like wind through a pipe.

He wanted to shoot it, but hesitated. He had the oddest sense that it was sentient, intelligent. He could not know how its kind had come to be here, maybe it wasn't even native to the earth, but he was certain it was a thinking creature. There was no doubt in his mind that it possessed an intelligent brain. It could reason. Maybe it was a cold, remorseless brain devoid of sympathy and pity, but he was certain it was smart.

Maybe even smarter than he was.

As he watched it watch him, its flesh went from that pale cream color to a shiny pink and then darkened, becoming yellow and orange, finally red as a boiled lobster and purple like a bruise. Then, yes, then it went green…emerald and jade and lime and olive, it mimicked perfectly the blotchy leafage of Indochina's tropical jungle.

A chameleon.

Yes, of course. That's how it hunted through the trees. Its camouflage was so entirely perfect, you could've walked right past it and never knew what it really was.

*No, no, it's much more than that,* he thought. *There's a language in its color changes. It's trying to communicate something, something important, something it wants us to know. If it wanted to kill us, it would have done so by now. It's curious and it knows we're curious. It's trying to relay something to me.*

The colors were changing faster now, indigo and violet, aquamarine and cerulean and scarlet, dozens of vibrant hues in-between.

"Fuck this," Comanche Jim said, bringing up his MAT-49.

"No!" Spiers cried.

Too late. Comanche Jim fired a volley of rounds at the creature, all of which hit it. It let out an enraged *SSSSKRRREEEEEK!* that was so loud Spiers' ears hurt.

It moved.

It darted forward incredibly fast, making a weird keening sound, those pods at its legs hissing and letting loose a storm of writhing silk.

The webs exploded around Wick before he could do so much as kiss his ass goodbye. They consumed him like coiling white snakes that branched out into dozens of strands that branched again and again and again. He was cocooned in seconds, then yanked back beneath the beast. Spiers saw that there was a great black slit on its underside that was opening like a vagina and that it was crowded with countless pink, puckering suckers that opened and closed like mouths, greedy to clamp onto something.

They found Wick.

Tangled in those rotting skeins of silk, he suddenly went rigid and there was a busy, rending sound like a wet/dry vac working a drenched carpet. The suckers went from bubble gum-pink to a livid red and Wick deflated like a balloon, literally collapsing into himself like a crushed aluminum can in nightmarish, cartoon-like speed.

By then, both Spiers and Comanche Jim were shouting and opening up on that big, ugly mother with their weapons and drilling channels into it. It knew pain, you could see that, for it let out a deafening, screeching noise and began to slip back into the chasm.

But Comanche Jim would not let it go.

He went right at it with his machete, hacking and chopping and then he was sprayed with crawling webs and the thing disappeared with him, too.

Spiers just sat there, his brain gone to mush.

*We might have had a chance,* he thought. *It didn't like us and it might have even hated us, but it wanted us to know something and now we'll never know what that was.*

Flashlight and weapon in hands, shaking his head from side to side, he just waited there while his heart tried to pound its way out of his chest. He knew he was insane. He had to be. Because a sane man would have run, climbed up and out of the mound. But he inched closer to the funnel and looked down there, scanning it with his light.

It was honeycombed far below.

He could see that much.

The entire passage opened up into some immense chamber that was honeycombed with dozens and dozens of cells like the hive of a wasp or bee. It dropped down and down and there was nothing but more of those oval cells as far as the light could reach.

He didn't see the creature or any of the others.

But he could hear Comanche Jim crying out down there, making muffled noises like his mouth was stuffed with wet leaves.

*You can't really be considering this.*

But he was. Something in him demanded it. Drawing in a sharp breath, Spiers began to climb down.

It wasn't hard going, the walls were made of a sticky material and set with a netting of webs. The going was quite easy like climbing down a net, but still he lowered himself carefully, carefully. He began to discover one horror after the other in his search for Comanche Jim. Each cell—or most of them—was stuffed with the partially-cocooned body of a man, woman, or child. Sometimes more than one. Some were skeletons covered in leathery flesh that had been there decades. Others were pale, but alive, their minds long gone in this madhouse. They looked through him and beyond. He saw the uniforms of Americans and Australians, NVA and Cambodians. Blackened stick-figures wore rotting, threadbare rags that must have been the uniforms of French colonial officers and the Foreign Legion. He even saw what looked to be several samurai swords that must have belonged to Japanese officers of World War II. There were dozens and dozens of mummies covered in dust and he couldn't even guess how long they had been there.

He came across a cell with an NVA soldier in it. His face was stark and wide-eyed, perfectly mad. There were several great tumorous growths on his throat. But as Spiers looked closer, he saw they were more of the gray ticks. Their bodies were pulsing as they sipped the soldier's blood.

The honeycomb was a great silent morgue tucked away here all these years by entities from out of space and time and reality.

He came across a web of glistening silk. There were several of the flies in it, but shrunken and dead. As he prodded the strands with the muzzle of his MAT-49, half a dozen of the ticks came crawling out to investigate.

*It's like some fucked-up ecosystem,* he found himself thinking. *There's things here that aren't anywhere else. Every crawling, leggy nightmare you can imagine is here in this place...how can that be?*

It was a question that kept rolling and rolling through his brain, even though he was trying to stay focused so his fear of this terrible place did not overwhelm him and destroy his nerve to go on, to see this through. Regardless, it needed answering. The whole damn valley was like nowhere else on Earth and the mound seemed to be the core of it, the blood-swelling heart of this hot, sticky, webby womb that was giving birth to horrors that had no right being in the first place.

What did it all mean?

Good God, what could it possibly mean?

It all whirled about in his head...the flies, the ticks, the spider-things—what the fuck did it all mean?

He paused about thirty feet down and looked around. The beam of his flashlight was filled with vaporous tendrils of mist that came from a central pit below filled with decay and bones and filth. Things were crawling in that putrescent soup: worming, slithering things that he did not want to know about.

He finally found Comanche Jim's cell.

He crawled in there, chopping through a lattice of web. He began to cut him free and Comanche Jim, tough man that he was, was barely holding it together. The thing had not drank from him, but it had touched him and the desire to go stark, raving mad was nearly irresistible.

"...*fucker...motherfucker,*" he was saying, shivering and shaking like his flesh was full of bugs. *"It touched me, man, that fucking thing touched me...oh it's so filthy...so cold and slippery...ahhhh...."*

He could talk, but he could not move. He was paralyzed. His limbs were like rubber.

Spiers heard movement and paused.

He looked out of the cell and shined his light.

He could see it.

One of the creatures was climbing back up now, its tail hovering above it like the stinger of a scorpion. It moved in leaps and bounds, darting up ten feet like a funnel web spider, then pausing, waiting, darting up again. He was pretty certain it was the one they had shot.

It was working its way back up from the pit, pausing by cells and drawing out people wrapped in shrouds of webs and vampirizing them, drinking from them as they screamed and howled and shook. It put them back in their cells like a child examining her collection of dolls. It webbed them back up and did something to them that made them stop moving.

Just like Comanche Jim.

Spiers figured it was stinging them, paralyzing them like a wasp does to a spider or a caterpillar.

He knew then what it was like for these poor bastards. They were kept here as food, injected with some toxin to keep them from escaping. The creatures came out of that pit below and sucked their blood, just enough to get by, taking good care of their livestock and then going up, up, out of the burrow and into the treetops to hunt men for their collection.

He clamped his jaw shut so he would not whimper as he heard those people below moaning as the thing drew off their life with moist, sucking sounds.

It was coming, working its way up and Comanche Jim was paralyzed, made of rubber. He could not get out and Spiers knew he couldn't carry him. He stripped his pack off him and pulled out the LAW rocket launcher, slung it over his shoulder.

Comanche Jim looked at him with a wild, imploring look that said, *oh please, oh Jesus, don't leave me here, kill me, kill me, kill me for God's sake, but don't let it touch me, don't let it…*

But it was too late.

In the flashlight beam, Spiers could see the creature waiting there, filling the opening. The chemical stench of the thing made his head whirl, it submerged the cell in a vaporous fetid heat. There was another smell, too, up close like that, a sharp, septic sort of stink. But he couldn't be sure whether it was coming from the beast or Comanche Jim himself.

It was too late to turn the flashlight off.

It knew where he was.

It must have.

Yet, he wasn't sure if it was looking at him or Comanche Jim. Its chambered face pulsated, filling and deflating like an air sack. The vertical lips opened like drapes being pulled, revealing the circle of its glossy eyes which were the size of tennis balls, a glimmering, kaleidoscopic golden flecked with green. Perfectly alien in all ways. The ring of gnashing yellow teeth scraped against one another and then parted, a black cavity of a mouth revealed beneath. It squirmed with fleshy things, suckers and tongues. The perfectly awful and hideous thing was that there were three other tiny mouths set in a triangular formation beyond the eyes. They had suckering lips and tiny hooked teeth.

Then its tail was in the cell like a monstrous, colorless earthworm. It moved across Spiers, who pressed himself into the corner, and found Comanche Jim. A quick jab and the hooked appendages injected neurotoxins into him. His eyes rolled back white.

Spiers saw how it fed.

Using its mandibles, it pulled Comanche Jim's numb body to it. The eyes disappeared behind heavy membranes and the smaller mouths took hold of him as the main mouth suctioned itself to his throat and began to drain the blood from him. The sounds were revolting, appalling…like a child sipping from a cup, licking and slurping. Comanche Jim's face contorted in a deranged, blubbering mask and his eyes bulged and drool ran from his mouth…and then it was over.

He was stuffed back in the cell and cocooned in silk.

The thing disappeared.

Spiers couldn't believe it. Maybe it didn't know he was there. Maybe its eyes didn't register light the way his own did, maybe it saw in a totally different spectrum. And maybe it just wanted Comanche Jim.

*Sorry, man, but you're beyond help.*

He climbed out of the cell and picked his way up, refusing to think about Comanche Jim or his staring, filmed eyes and mottled flesh, mouth hooked in a silent, terrible scream.

He moved upwards slowly, greasy with sweat, the feel of the webs making his hands simultaneously itch and sting and he wondered, not for the first time, if contact with them might be causing his skin some permanent damage. Now and again, his fingers broke through a weak, delicate plaiting of web and he touched the material beneath. He expected it to be dirt or rock but it was neither. It felt like a sort of pliable plastic, warm to the touch, and he was certain he could feel a sort of subtle movement beneath it that made him quickly draw away his hand.

*Like living tissue,* he thought. *That's what you were thinking.*

But if it was, he refused to consider it. There were too many questions and now was not the time to answer them. There was only survival; he could not think beyond that right now.

And below, movement.

Spiers climbed faster and faster, ever aware of that pit of slime and rot far below. He could hear the beast coming up after him now, thinking one of its prey had escaped. He climbed and climbed, pulling himself up and up as the thing raced after him until his hands found the lip of the chasm and he was out of the funnel itself. By then, the thing was so close its stink filled him with waves of nausea.

He rolled and came up with his back against a sticky wall of webs like cheesecloth behind him. He lodged the flashlight between his knees and unslung the LAW rocket launcher. It was a disposable, one-use weapon. A two-foot olive green tube. He pulled the pin and it opened to its full thirty-six inches. He took aim, finger on the trigger.

He thought: *One chance, one chance, you don't kill it, you become like the others...*

It came over the lip of the chasm twenty feet away and hung there, those jointed legs clicking, its body inflating and deflating like it was breathing. It was coated in those stringy webs and filaments of them drifted out like hairs full of static electricity. The chromatophores that fired its pigmentation turned it a juicy pink and then a brilliant orange. Its puckering face sucked in and out, teeth sliding from the gums.

"COME ON!" Spiers shouted at it. "COME AND GET SOME!"

It launched itself forward with a squealing, squeaking sound...a storm of silk exploding from it, its tail coming around for the kill...and Spiers pulled the trigger. There was a momentary blinding explosion as the rocket erupted from the tube and then a gigantic, rending explosion as it found its target and the thing came apart like a bag of meat, wet flesh and stinking ichor spraying in every possible direction. Spiers was hit by both the shock wave and the thing's remains and it knocked him six feet and pulled the air from his lungs.

He came to a few seconds later and the thing was dead, exploded to fragments. Nothing left but oceans of brown-green blood and burning sections of exoskeleton.

He was covered in its filth and the chasm was on fire. All those webs had lit up from the burning shrapnel and the place was going up, nature finally unleashed and wiping out this madness, engulfing it in flames.

Spiers crawled out of there as the fire spread closer and closer, bathed in a hot, singed stink like burning hair. Then he found the dangling ropes and climbed up and out.

Free.

Ƅ

He lay there, panting in the hot sun as black, greasy smoke poured from the tunnel behind him. He laid there for some time, smoking and trying to screw his head on straight. The creature was not one of a kind. There were others, many others. Some were trapped in the mound, but others were in the jungle and they would be coming now.

He couldn't be here when they returned.

He grabbed up Wick's pack, abandoning his own and checked the contents quickly, making sure the crystal radio was there along with the gridded maps. Okay. He grabbed up his weapons and moved to the edge of the mound.

"Shit," he heard himself say.

The jungle down there was a living thing, moving and rustling and creeping as hordes of the creatures broke free of the brush like army ants on the march. They were all returning to the mound now. It was under attack and they were rushing to its defense, trilling and screeching.

Spiers ran around the mound and saw them coming from all sides. There was only one thing to do. It was crazy and it was suicidal but it was all he had. He located a section of the hillside where the vegetation was thick and tangled with human remains and the creatures had not yet burst from the forest.

He lowered himself down about half way and crawled beneath a multitude of vines and squeezed himself amongst bones—jawless skulls and ribcages and leg staves.

The creatures were coming.

Their combined stench was nauseating.

The sound of their shrilling cries, *ssskreek! ssskreek! ssskreek!* set his nerves on edge and echoed around in his skull. Then they were pouring over him, clicking and whirring and scraping. After maybe a minute—a very long and horrible minute—they were gone.

He'd gotten away with it.

He'd really gotten away with it.

Quickly, he climbed down the rest of the way, tripping and falling and rolling, then scrambling through razor grass that tore his arms and jumping over stumps and fallen trees and then he was in the heavy, coveting shadows of the jungle.

The sun was beginning to set.

He broke free into a clearing and sighted the highest hill he could find that was maybe a quarter mile or so away. He fought forward, stumbling and running, barely staying on his feet. He was done in, exhausted, but he had to keep going.

*"You got to keep pushing, cherry,"* he could hear Carmody saying, the voice weary and nearly sympathetic. *"Too close to the end now. Do not fold-up and do not give in. E and E your ass out of here."*

"Sure, Gunny. You can count on me."

There was something funny there but Spiers was too damn fatigued to recognize it. He was a stumbling, bumbling, wind-up toy, a tin soldier revolving in ever-weakening circles. Though outwardly he kept going, inside, at his very core, there was an exhaustion that was beyond bone-deep, it corrupted his foundation, a knot of rock-hard black paralysis that was pressing outwards, rendering muscles and joints and ligaments and nerve endings useless. His brain felt like a burned out fuse. His body was a flaccid mass of tissue. His eyes kept glazing over, needing to shut, to cancel out the world if only for a few minutes and drift in dark fuzz. Even his breathing was slow and labored. He reached out to fear (his constant companion) but it was no longer there; it had been replaced by numb acceptance which, in a combat zone, is one step away from being zipped in a body bag and he knew it. *You hear about that sniper name of Spiers? Fucker went out with Force Recon night-stalkers on a full-blooded Stingray and found himself in a nest of monsters. Then you know what that diddy-bopping cherry-assed muther did? He froze up. He got too tired and too weak and he just said, awwww, fuck it, poor me, poor little old me, and laid down and died. Hearts and flowers, Spear-chucker, hearts and flowers—*

Spiers realized that he had stopped, that he was leaning up against the rugged bark of an ancient wind-bent tree. Not only that, but he had plugged a cigarette in his mouth and he was pulling off it with slow, easy drags like some guy back home that had just finished his chops and mashed potatoes and apple pie and had stepped out onto the back porch for a smoke and some breeze. Amazing. Utterly amazing.

The knowledge of this did not energize him.

No, it made him feel even more used up. He slid down to the ground, smoking, not thinking, realizing he was having trouble distinguishing the tactile difference between his filthy, ragged jungle fatigues and his own skin. They had become one, they had grown together. Oily, loose, threadbare. As he looked off in the direction of the setting sun, feeling its golden heat on his sunburned cheeks one last time before the chill of the tropical night turned his own sweat into a clammy shroud, his eyes were bloodshot and red-rimmed. His skin was pale beyond pale. His lips were tinged gray. The only color on him was dirt, grime, and the swelling knobs of insect bites that freckled his neck and cheeks.

He had gone crazy.

In the most horrendous combat zone imaginable, he had gone fucking crazy. Of all things. The realization of that made him feel like he was tripping his brains out. But he had to shake it, and when he did he was moving. Or was he hallucinating? No, he was moving, one foot in front of the other, carrying himself with forward momentum. Just like at Parris Island when he was so tired he couldn't take another step. Yes, he was doing it, he was really doing it.

When he reached the hill, he climbed using vines and roots to drag himself up with. When he got to the top, it was nearly dark out. In his mind, the same words repeated themselves again and again: *Tango Ten-Five. Green Garden. Orange smoke. Papa Nickel.* He was scratched and bleeding, his body aching. Sweat ran down his face. Insects crawled over him and leeches had suckered themselves to his arms and neck. A fat brown spider raced over the back of his hand. But he wouldn't give in, not yet.

He dug the radio out of Wick's pack and set it up before it was too dark.

That's when he heard the resounding siren-like call he had heard before. It was loud and insistent, droning from the direction of the mound. What Amoro had said sounded like a hunting horn.

The ground began to tremble.

He knew what it was; it could only be one thing.

*Not again, not again.*

The gigantic unknown thing that had stalked them in the jungle was coming back again. He was certain it was coming for him. That this was all about to become very personal, very private and intimate in the worst possible way.

*Call in the airstrike, dumbass. Rain Armageddon down just like Wick told you.*

But he couldn't.

He was afraid to move and even more afraid to speak. The ground vibrated, sticks and leaves falling from trees overhead as that thing got closer and closer, bearing down on him to squash him flat. Trees were falling. More than falling, he realized. They sounded like they were being felled by axes, split in half, broken, stomped, shattered. The world was trembling, the ground shivering like soft mud.

He smelled the stink of the thing, that mephitic overpowering green stench of putrescence that he had earlier acquainted with rotting animal hides but now, in closer proximity, smelled of mass graves and plague pits maggoty with unburied pox-blackened corpses.

The stench turned his stomach, but more so it made something inside him, something at his very nucleus, wither and curl-up. And he realized that the thing that was coming for him was more than just physically and organically obscene, but spiritually noxious. That its presence not only made him want to vomit his guts out, but to scratch his eyes from their sockets and slit his wrists until hot freshets of blood gushed scarlet down his arms.

This thing could not only destroy you, it could tear your mind out by the roots if you looked at it.

*Don't let me see! Don't let me look on it! Don't let me know what it is,* he pleaded with some higher power even though the brutality and carnage of war had long ago destroyed whatever faith struggled feebly inside him.

But now he was willing to believe.

He was willing to embrace any god that would come to his aid.

It was closer now.

The low perpetual humming of it was so loud that he couldn't hear anything else. It moved through his body, making him feel like he was vibrating inside. The trees around him rattled like bones. The droning was the backdrop to the other sound the thing made, that crackling/grinding noise that reminded him of immense industrial gears threshing.

The world shook and he realized that the creature was not coming for him at all; no, it was heading in the direction of the mound. It would pass very close by, though, in the cut between this hill and the next.

He waited.

He shook.

The sunset was painting the hilltops with blood. Terror lived in him, sliding through him and taking hold of his guts and dragging them up into his chest.

Now the beast was in view.

It made a huge, roaring, brain-jarring sort of cry like a tube train rushing past a station and he knew if he looked up, he would see it in the dying light, he would see something that would never leave his nightmares.

But he had to see.

He had to look.

And he did.

He saw something immense and scaly and iridescent-green surge past the hill he stood on with the gelatinous sort of locomotion of an amoeba. It bubbled with liquid flesh. It slithered and oozed and undulated, sixty feet tall with what looked like dozens upon dozens of long coiling limbs that clawed over the ground and knocked trees aside and snaked high into the sky above. That grinding/clicking sound was created by a series of carapace-like plates that covered it like armor and were constantly in motion, turning and grating against one another but never wholly still. They were set with something like yawning, immense mouths that exhaled a scalding wind that withered the leaves on the trees and created that constant humming noise. In the twilight, of course, he could not be sure of anything, not really, but he saw it had another mouth, something like an immense chasm that opened and closed with a puckering, juicy sound.

Then it disappeared in the dusk and he was only aware of its shape—which was profuse and impossible—and the terrible booming tread of its limbs.

*Call it in.*

*Call in that airstrike.*

Yes, he clutched the crystal radio tightly, ready to make the call…but something was happening. As darkness came down, there was a sound of thunder and a booming that echoed through the valley and he knew without a doubt it was coming from the mound. Yes, he saw branching arcs of blue lightning rising up from it into the sky where they connected into a raging network of forking electricity that made the horizon glow with a green pulsing fire. The energy built and built and it was like a static charge crawling over his arms and down his spine. The sky was filled with wild blue-green auroras that flickered and flashed, licking down to the mound itself in a solid luminous emanation of radiance.

Then the earth beneath him shook and the hillside rolled with a shivering jelly-like motion and in the brightness that actually seemed to burn his eyes, he saw that the mound was shaking itself loose of the jungle, rising up and up, abandoning the hillside that covered it. Huge cracks appeared in the ground and from each there was a smoldering light and rising plumes of white steam. And then the hillside exploded in a rain of debris and he saw something like a sphere rising up into the night. It was a gigantic thing that seemed to get larger and larger as it revealed itself. It looked like some shining cyclopean egg that was chambered with shiny oval lenses like the portholes of an antique bathysphere. Huge sections of earth clung to it along with trees and sections of rock, all of which began to drop free as it continued to emerge.

*You know what that is, don't you?* a voice in the back of Spiers' head said to him. *You know what you're looking at?*

And he did and he didn't.

Whatever it was, the very concept was too much for his simple brain and he could not hope to comprehend the significance of what he was seeing or what it might mean. Physically, the sphere had to be easily half a mile in circumference if not a great deal more. He had been inside it, but he realized then that he had barely been within the periphery of the thing. Its size was truly beyond the scope of his imagination.

Calling in an airstrike against something like that was ludicrous. Besides, there was no way any fixed-wing aircraft would make it way out here before it was gone.

This is what Wick had kept from him.

The real nature of this operation.

The very thing that required an Omega clearance.

It finally broke free of the hillside and the crazy electrical activity in the sky died out as if a switch had been thrown. It hovered there, casting violent storm winds in every direction, tree roots hanging from it like tentacles. It made a sharp, crackling sort of sound and tongues of lightning shot out from it, one of them striking a massive cypress tree and splitting it open in an eruption of cold blue fire. It was glowing white by then, searing plumes of smoke and steam rising from it. It looked like some enormous, slowly-rotating melting white-hot mass. Then it rose into the sky and the illumination died out and the pitch black of the jungle returned. For a few seconds, it looked like a bright full moon in the sky and then nothing but another star in the heavens and then it winked out completely.

Spiers sat there for the longest time, just smoking and trying to make sense of it all and wondering if it had all been some insane fever dream. When Amoro said the siren call had been like a hunting horn, he had immediately thought that the valley was maybe like a private hunting preserve and maybe it had been at that. But where had the spider things and their numerous pets come from? The sphere had been encased in the earth and something like that would have taken centuries, if not thousands of years.

It was some kind of hunting trip, all right.

Yet…there was a logic to it. He couldn't grasp it completely, but some of it made sense. The sphere had come here perhaps centuries before and the valley had indeed been a hunting preserve. The spider things were the intelligence behind it. The colossal green thing was like a herder, driving the quarry towards the hunters. The ticks were probably just a pesty form of parasite that hitched a ride. The Viets and their attendant flies were probably something along the line of gamekeepers—

Oh Christ, the madness of it could have gone on and on. The bottom line is that those creatures were not from this world and giving them human motivations was probably a mistake. He would never know what it was all about and that was probably a good thing.

He dug in Wick's pack and got the maps out of their plastic pouch. Using his lighter, he gridded out his location and got on the radio. *"Green Garden, Green Garden, this is Tango Ten-Five requesting extraction…"* He repeated the message three times over the next five minutes. After that, it was really just a matter of hoping the FAC picked up his transmission so he could pop orange smoke for the chopper that would hoist him out of the jungle. If things worked out, he'd be taking a shower and drinking cold beer in a few hours. If they didn't work out, he had one evil motherfucker of a hike ahead of him. So he waited there on that lonely hillside in the primeval vastness of the valley, staring up into the star-filled sky and the immense cosmos beyond and wondered, just wondered, his simple primate brain open to limitless possibilities it had never even considered before.

THE END

www.ingramcontent.com/pod-product-compliance
Lightning Source LLC
Chambersburg PA
CBHW051954170626
46808CB00007B/2617